"You Don't Want To Hear It? Tough.

"You asked the question, Mr. Sheriff Jericho Rivers, so you're going to know who my lovers were. You're going to hear how they looked, and how they made me feel."

Maria could've sworn his handsome, weathered face paled.

As her body responded to his heated, possessive look, she caught back an unsteady sigh and launched into her answer.

"My legion of lovers are all of a type. All are kind. Gentle. All dark, stronger than the strongest oak and taller than the sky. They all have eyes as silvery gray as a stormy sea. And they come to me in the night, wherever I am. Africa. Egypt. China. Russia. Belle Terre.

"They come to me only in my wishes and my dreams." Her free hand trailed over his jaw, her fingertips lingered at his mouth. "Because all my lovers are you, Jericho. Wherever I am, wherever I go, only you."

Dear Reader,

The year 2000 has been a special time for Silhouette, as we've celebrated our 20th anniversary. Readers from all over the world have written to tell us what they love about our books, and we'd like to share with you part of a letter from Carolyn Dann of Grand Bend, Ontario, who's a fan of Silhouette Desire. Carolyn wrote, "I like the storylines…the characters…the front covers… All the characters in the books are the kind of people you like to read about. They're all down-to-earth, everyday people." And as a grand finale to our anniversary year, Silhouette Desire offers six of your favorite authors for an especially memorable month's worth of passionate, powerful, provocative reading!

We begin the lineup with the always wonderful Barbara Boswell's MAN OF THE MONTH, *Irresistible You,* in which a single woman nine months pregnant meets her perfect hero while on jury duty. The incomparable Cait London continues her exciting miniseries FREEDOM VALLEY with *Slow Fever.* Against a beautiful Montana backdrop, the oldest Bennett sister is courted by a man who spurned her in their teenage years. And *A Season for Love,* in which Sheriff Jericho Rivers regains his lost love, continues the new miniseries MEN OF BELLE TERRE by beloved author BJ James.

Don't miss the thrilling conclusion to the Desire miniseries FORTUNE'S CHILDREN: THE GROOMS in Peggy Moreland's *Groom of Fortune.* Elizabeth Bevarly will delight you with *Monahan's Gamble.* And *Expecting the Boss's Baby* is the launch title of Leanne Banks's new miniseries, MILLION DOLLAR MEN, which offers wealthy, philanthropic bachelors guaranteed to seduce you.

We hope all readers of Silhouette Desire will treasure the gift of this special month.

Happy holidays!

Joan Marlow Golan

Joan Marlow Golan
Senior Editor, Silhouette Desire

Please address questions and book requests to:
Silhouette Reader Service
U.S.: 3010 Walden Ave., P.O. Box 1325, Buffalo, NY 14269
Canadian: P.O. Box 609, Fort Erie, Ont. L2A 5X3

A Season for Love
BJ JAMES

Published by Silhouette Books
America's Publisher of Contemporary Romance

To my parents, with love

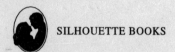 SILHOUETTE BOOKS

ISBN 0-373-76335-2

A SEASON FOR LOVE

Copyright © 2000 by BJ James

This edition published by arrangement with Harlequin Books S.A.

Visit Silhouette at www.eHarlequin.com

Printed in U.S.A.

Books by BJ James

Silhouette Desire

The Sound of Goodbye #332
Twice in a Lifetime #396
Shiloh's Promise #529
Winter Morning #595
Slade's Woman #672
A Step Away #692
Tears of the Rose #709
*The Man with the
   Midnight Eyes* #751
Pride and Promises #789
Another Time, Another Place #823
The Hand of an Angel #844
*Heart of the Hunter #945
*The Saint of Bourbon Street #951
*A Wolf in the Desert #956
†Whispers in the Dark #1081
†Journey's End #1106
†Night Music #1286
‡The Return of Adams Cade #1309
‡A Season for Love #1335

Silhouette Intimate Moments

Broken Spurs #733

Silhouette Books

World's Most Eligible Bachelors
†*Agent of the Black Watch*

*Men of the Black Watch
†The Black Watch
‡Men of Belle Terre

BJ JAMES'

first book for Silhouette Desire was published in February 1987. Her second Desire garnered for BJ a second Maggie, the coveted award of the Georgia Romance Writers. Through the years there have been other awards and nominations for awards, including, from *Romantic Times Magazine,* Reviewer's Choice, Career Achievement, Best Desire and Best Series Romance of the Year. In that time, her books have appeared regularly on a number of bestseller lists, among them Waldenbooks and *USA Today.*

On a personal note, BJ and her physician husband have three sons and two grandsons. While her address reads Mooreboro, this is only the origin of a mail route passing through the countryside. A small village set in the foothills of western North Carolina is her home.

IT'S OUR 20th ANNIVERSARY!
December 2000 marks the end of our anniversary year.
We hope you've enjoyed the many special titles already
offered, and we invite you to sample those wonderful titles
on sale this month! 2001 promises to be every bit as
exciting, so keep coming back to Silhouette Books,
where love comes alive....

Desire

 #1333 Irresistible You
Barbara Boswell

 #1334 Slow Fever
Cait London

#1335 A Season for Love
BJ James

#1336 Groom of Fortune
Peggy Moreland

#1337 Monahan's Gamble
Elizabeth Bevarly

 **#1338 Expecting the
Boss's Baby**
Leanne Banks

Romance

 **#1486 Sky's Pride and
Joy**
Sandra Steffen

#1487 Hunter's Vow
Susan Meier

 **#1488 Montana's Feisty
Cowgirl**
Carolyn Zane

#1489 Rachel and the M.D.
Donna Clayton

**#1490 Mixing Business...with
Baby**
Diana Whitney

#1491 His Special Delivery
Belinda Barnes

Special Edition

#1363 The Delacourt Scandal
Sherry Woods

#1364 The McCaffertys: Thorne
Lisa Jackson

 **#1365 The Cowboy's
Gift-Wrapped Bride**
Victoria Pade

Rumor Has It... **#1366 Lara's Lover**
Penny Richards

#1367 Mother in a Moment
Allison Leigh

#1368 Expectant Bride-To-Be
Nikki Benjamin

Intimate Moments

#1045 Special Report
Merline Lovelace/Maggie Price/
Debra Cowan

a year of loving dangerously **#1046 Strangers When We
Married**
Carla Cassidy

**#1047 A Very...Pregnant
New Year's**
Doreen Roberts

#1048 Mad Dog and Annie
Virginia Kantra

#1049 Mirror, Mirror
Linda Randall Wisdom

#1050 Everything But a Husband
Karen Templeton

One

He watched her.

From a small alcove above the atrium of the sprawling museum, he could see every patron and every celebrant, read the nuance of each gesture or expression. But it was only she who had the power to captivate. Only this woman who fascinated.

As he watched, music and laughter filled the grand hall from marble floor to gold leaf ceiling. Dancers, resplendent beneath the light of 18th-century chandeliers, reflected in one ornate mirror after another. Antique blue satin draping doors opening onto small galleries shimmered as darkly as the sea beyond.

The atrium was magnificent, an exquisite replica of the past the very cliquish Southern town of Belle Terre revered. In all its rich, Low Country grandeur, this was the heart of the museum, the piéce de résistance. An ironic setting for the beautiful woman.

There was a time she wouldn't have been welcome. Venerable denizens greeting her familiarly tonight wouldn't have spoken to her on the street. Men strutting in dusted-off tuxedos, lusting for a word or a smile, in the past lusted only for her nubile body.

She'd been brutalized and reviled by Belle Terre. Yet she moved among its self-appointed aristocracy graciously, as if she were one of them and had always been.

Politely refusing hors d'oeuvres, flutes of champagne, and invitations to dance by the dozens, she accepted the fawning acclaim, yet remained quietly aloof. In a gown that flowed like liquid gold about her, tastefully revealing the qualities that once sparked scorn and lechery, Maria Elena Delacroix, the outcast of Belle Terre, held court with the regal dignity of a queen.

Most of the men in the room were half in love with her. And one completely, irrevocably.

"Sheriff Rivers."

Turning at the sound of his name, Jericho Rivers found Harcourt Kerwin Hamilton IV, better known as Court, and more recently as Deputy Hamilton, poised on the top step of the curving stair. "Something wrong, Court?"

"No, sir." Moving to the sheriff's side, Court looked out over the atrium. "It's a grand affair. *Grandmère* says parties like this were common in her day."

Grandmère. Jericho smiled at the term, a part of the pretentious idiom of the historical coastal town. The only name he'd been allowed to call his own grandmother. "I imagine a lot of things that are rare now were commonplace in her day."

"But there's something that isn't commonplace in any day."

Because he'd been taught from birth that it was rude to point, Court only nodded. But even the nod was superfluous. Jericho hadn't a doubt Court's youthful gaze was as drawn to Maria Elena Delacroix as any male's in the room.

"My sister says you were friends of Ms. Delacroix in school. When she was part of your class at the academy."

Court was still in short pants when his sister was in high school—he wouldn't remember that Maria Elena was looked upon as the sort proper young girls of Belle Terre's society shunned. Jericho doubted the older sister ever deigned to speak to her. Most certainly there had been no friendship.

Even he hadn't been the friend he should have. Remembering how he had failed her, his voice was grim. "We knew her. All of us."

A smile of masculine appreciation firmly in place, Court's gaze followed the elegantly clad woman as she detached herself from the crowd, stepped between satin curtains, and disappeared into the darkness beyond. "With a face and body like that, she must have been the most popular girl in the whole school. But I bet none of you expected she would become a famous newscaster."

Jericho was silent as he remembered the sad young girl who sat apart in morning assembly and walked the halls of Belle Terre Academy alone. As the hurt, bruised look that had haunted him for years loomed in his mind, he replied in a low, thoughtful voice, "I don't think any of us knew what to expect of Ms. Delacroix." After a long moment he added, "We still don't."

Court Hamilton was like an eager puppy. Too exuberant, too excitable, and far too inquisitive. "It's good to have her back, though. Isn't it?"

Was it? Jericho wondered as he pondered the consequences of her return. What dormant fear had she wakened? What upheaval would this single night bring to settled lives? Who would suffer or profit most, the denizens of Belle Terre, or she?

Angry for the past, distracted by contemplations of the near future, he lashed out when he shouldn't have. "Is that why you came up here, Hamilton? To gossip?"

Beyond a puzzled look, Court Hamilton did not react to the rare barb. "No, sir. I came to take a turn here in the crow's nest. I thought there might be some folk you would like to speak with before the last dance."

Ignoring Hamilton's joking title for the alcove, Jericho

glanced at his watch. It was almost midnight. The celebration would be ending shortly.

"Thank you, Court." Jericho Rivers smiled, rancor gone, but with no humor touching his calm gray gaze. "There is someone."

Descending the stairs with the distinctive and uncommon agility of an extraordinary athlete, despite a ravaged knee, in seconds he was paused on the landing. Towering above the tallest of the celebrants by inches, his thick, dark hair gleaming with the soft sheen of coal, in the spinning kaleidoscope of lights, the sheriff of Belle Terre stood observing the crowd.

Unlike Maria Delacroix, he was one of them by birth. Born into the mystique of the merit and excellence of history, a scion of influence and old money. Schooled in charm and gallantry, as handsome as Lucifer, as magnetic, he could have been the prince of society. Yet he held himself apart. Apart from the pretenses, from the bluster and posturing. Apart and immune even from the playful flirtations of its polished, sophisticated femmes fatales.

Handsome as sin, yet aloof. Indeed, he was an intriguing enigma, an everlasting challenge. But tonight, as his silver-gray gaze moved over the crowd, there was an unapproachable look about him that discouraged even the most persistent of covetous ladies.

When the slow, steady perusal was done, his concern for any breach of security in these last minutes of the gala was allayed. Only then did he move through the throng, a distinguished figure with an air of authority. His formal wear draping the striking breadth of his shoulders and the deep musculature of his chest only a bit more impeccably than the khaki uniform of his standard daily wear. Given his size, his astounding presence, and the look of haunting secrets in his level gray gaze, the merrymakers gave way as if he were a human tide.

Crossing the marble floor quickly, speaking pleasantly but

abruptly disengaging himself from any insistent conversations, Jericho didn't pause until he reached an open door.

As he stood, remembering, the orchestra finished the last of a Cole Porter classic. One of his favorites. He didn't notice.

Into the lull, almost too quietly to be heard, he murmured, ''Good evening, Maria Elena.''

Two

"Is it really, Sheriff Rivers?" She stood alone on the small gallery, her back to him, her hands gripping the massive balustrade the only sign of tension. The only sign that she waited for him. "A good evening, I mean."

She faced him, her smile rueful, provocative. With the moonlit sea at her back and the wind teasing tendrils of midnight hair about her shoulders, she was the stuff of dreams and old memories.

"Pleasant enough." Moving from the doorway, leaving the pomp and revelry of the gala behind him, Jericho crossed the shadowed space separating them. The scent of her perfume mingled with the night. A blended fragrance of sultry intoxication.

As he stood by her side, looking out at the surf, her cheek nearly brushed his shoulder. Tilting her head, she spoke softly. "It's been a long time, Jericho."

"Yes." The word fell like a stone between them. With the

music quieted, only the rhythm of distant waves washing over the shore breached a wall of silence.

The pale globe of a full moon rode low over the surf, its reflected light a river of silver brightening the night. Remembering the times he'd watched the same view from his own gallery with his mind wandering to the girl she'd been, Jericho waited. Feeling her gaze moving over him, contemplating, analyzing, he didn't act or react. The first move would be hers.

Fronds of a palm brushed against a nearby wall. Rigging of beached sailboats clanked against masts. The engines of a freighter, barely a lighted dot against the horizon, thrummed for a moment on a gust, then faded into nothing as it passed.

As suddenly as it began, the muted cacophony ceased. Leaving behind a silence aching to be broken.

"I never expected to see you here again," she said, at last, as the band played the first measure of "Goodnight Ladies."

"I never expected I would return to Belle Terre."

"Nor did I."

Laughing a breathy laugh, she shook her head. "Jericho Rivers, young Goliath and rare friend, still a man of few words."

Shifting slightly, with his hand resting on the heavy iron of the gallery railing, from his great height he looked down at her. "What would you have me say, Maria Elena?"

"I'm not sure."

"Why did you come?" His voice was deep, as mild as the night. As intriguing.

"This was an assignment. Only an assignment."

"The opening of a museum devoted to the history of a small coastal town?" he scoffed. "Hardly a noteworthy event. Certainly nothing to merit the attention of a famous news personality."

"Human interest, Jericho. The history of Belle Terre and its reverence for the past constitute human interest."

"Ah-hh, of course. That is your forte, the element that sets you apart in your work and your photography. So, when our tidbit of publicity happened to stray across a strategic desk, someone recalled Belle Terre was your hometown. And *voilá!*—you're here," he surmised quietly. "Is that how it went?"

"Something like that."

"You could have refused. Yet you didn't." There was a nuance of tenderness in his comment. Caught in a shaft of light, his face was barren of expression, but his gaze was turbulent.

The heat of that gaze reached into her, touching the secret, lonely places, waking needs and dreams she'd put aside. A gaze that set her heart beating so wildly, she feared it was visible beneath the clinging gown. Resting a hand on the curve of her shoulder, willing away tensions that had gathered and grown the whole evening, she moved her head in the barest denial. Her lips formed a silent no.

"Why? Why have you come, Maria Elena?" His voice dropped lower, even deeper. Yet the tone was no less compelling when he questioned again, "Why didn't you refuse?"

A cloud passed over the moon, in the pale darkness the sound of the sea seemed muted. In a voice in keeping with the hush, she began as if by rote, "Reporting news is my job. I don't choose the place. I simply go where it takes me. This time it brought me..."

Jericho moved closer, the subtle and familiar scent of him as compelling as his voice, as unsettling as a touch. Her tongue faltered on the beginning of a glib lie. The strange undercurrent in his questions, and a mood she didn't understand, simmered scarcely below a debonair veneer. Not sure how to respond or react, picking up a lost thread, she began again. "This time it brought me..."

"Home," he provided the word she never intended, in a voice unlike any she'd ever heard. The storm was gone from his gaze. The battle he'd fought with himself had ended. When he looked at her there was only tenderness. "Home to Belle Terre. Home to me."

"No!" Her denial was a strangled cry. The hand at her shoulder clenched and slipped to her breast. With a sweep of her lashes, shielding her from his riveting gaze, she turned her face away. A long breath shuddered through her, the pulse at her throat hammered as if her heart would race into madness. With a low moan, she lurched forward, desperate, intent on fleeing.

Maria was quick. Jericho was quicker. His hand flashed past her, closing, as the other, over the railing. Holding her in that imprisoning space, yet not touching her, he bent to her. "Stay."

"I can't." Her voice was low and unsteady. "The rest of the crew will be looking for me."

"To go back to the inn?" He moved another subtle step, his body brushed hers. The heat of him surrounded her. "To sleep alone?"

"Yes," she flung at him. "Alone!"

"That's what you want?" His left hand curled at her waist. With his right he turned her face to his. One gray gaze dueled with another. "Is it, truly, Mary Elena?"

Gathering courage, she glared into his probing stare. "I came to fulfill an assignment, Jericho, nothing more. When and with whom I sleep isn't a concern."

"Liar." The word had the ring of an endearment as his lips slanted in a patient smile. Looking away from her stormy scowl, his gaze moved down her throat to the shadowed cleft of her demure décolletage. "Isn't that why you wore a gown that clings like liquid gold and blazes like fire? Why have you waited alone on the gallery, except to drive me to this?"

"I came back to Belle Terre on assignment. Not home. Not to you." The litany of her denial fell from rigid lips. When she would have looked away again, the curve of his palm about her cheek stopped her. "Don't, Jericho." Anger blazed out of desperation. "I came to gather news. I don't want this. I...I don't want you."

"No?" He smiled in sympathy as she fought the battle he'd

fought for hours. His fingertips drifted down her cheek and throat to the pulsing hollow at its base. "Then what does this mean?"

Catching his roving fingers in hers, changing his focus and avoiding his question, with thumb and forefinger she turned the scarred and worn gold band he wore. "And this?" she whispered. "A wedding band, worn on your right hand? What does it mean?"

Closing his fist over hers, lifting their joined hands, he stroked the flesh of her wrists with his lips before he met her gaze again. "It means whatever you want it to mean, Maria Elena. As little or as much and for as long. Perhaps just for the night."

With a low sound that might have been laughter were it not for the raw note of pain, she leaned her forehead against his shoulder. "Damn you, Jericho. Damn you to hell and back. Eighteen years, and then this."

"I take that as a yes." Burying his hand in the dark wealth of her hair, sending the anchoring pins flying, he waited in simmering, barely contained impatience.

Raising her face to his, with her hair tumbling from the glamorous coiffeur as if it had waited as impatiently for his plundering caress, she whispered, "Yes." Then again, "Yes!"

Finding strength in fury and need, a whisper became a low cry: "Damn you, Jericho!" Hands sliding over his jacket and the smooth tucks of his shirt, she circled his nape with clasping fingers. Drawing his mouth to hers, she whispered. "In hell or heaven, after all the years, why is it always you? Always only Jericho, with no thought of tomorrow."

"Hell will come soon enough, my love." Sweeping her into his embrace, he pledged, "But for tonight, I promise only heaven."

Maria slept. Like a child too tired to toss or turn, she lay half curled on her side, her hair spread in dark rivulets over his pillow, a hand tucked beneath her chin. But it was more than a long night of unquenchable passion that caused the exhaustion marking her face and body. Far more than exhaustion that made her sleep too tense, too still, too guarded.

The first glint of dawn filtering into his bedroom woke him. Concern kept him sitting by the bed keeping watch as she slept. With each precious second, as the day grew older and first light touched the room, he worried it would disturb her. Yet he dared not risk the clatter of closing row after row of shutters.

Twice, while he watched, she frowned and tossed her head, muttering in a language he didn't understand. Twice he caught the sliding sheet, drawing it over her naked breasts again. Returning to his chair each time with the ache of desire, he knew wherever sleep had taken her, it wasn't to him and the night they shared.

"I want it all, sweetheart. The night, the day, your dreams. You, Maria Elena...waking or sleeping." His voice was hushed, though there was no one to hear.

Unable to resist temptation, he took her hand in his and was surprised when her frown faded. When, unconsciously soothed by his touch, the unnatural tension of her sleep grew restful, then serene. Lacing the fingers of both hands around hers, he leaned his forehead against them and closed his burning eyes.

Perhaps he slept, steeped in the scent of her, locked away from all but the muffled sounds of a world not yet awake. Perhaps he only slipped into waking dreams as he remembered the night, the darkness, the dusky room spangled with wisps of moonlight. Soft sighs and shuddering breaths. Wandering, wondering touches, hungering kisses lingering long and deep. Low sweet cries speaking more than words.

The caress of her body gliding over his. The tease of her swaying breasts as she leaned over him discovering the changes time and manhood had wrought in the boy who had been her first lover.

The fall of her tears as she kissed the pallid scars of too many surgeries on his knee. The catch in her breathing as he drew her from her exploration, cradling her breasts in his palms, cherishing nipples furled like new rosebuds with his lips and tongue.

In his drowsy, waking dream, he remembered the play of light and darkness veiling her in tantalizing mystery as her long legs twined about him. He would remember forever the thrust of her body accepting him, enfolding him, taking him deep inside her.

He remembered the clasping heat, the sweet caressing strokes soothing him, comforting him. Maria driving him mad with delight, with ecstasy. And as he'd dreamed she would one day, with love.

"Jericho?" The whispered word and the brush of fingertips skimming over his hair brought him back.

Lifting his head, his gaze collided with Maria's. Neither spoke. As her questing fingers grew still, neither moved.

After a moment, she smiled a contented smile. "Jericho."

Dropping a kiss on her knuckles, he said, "Good morning, Maria Elena."

Tracing the line of his lips, her smile softened. "Maria Elena. Only you call me that. To the rest of the world I'm simply Maria, and sometimes, Ms. Delacroix."

"What would you have me call you?"

"I like how you say my name." A wandering caress trailed from his face to the hands that encircled hers. Her smile wavered. "I thought I dreamed you."

"I'm real, my love."

"In a world of arrogant pretense, you were always my anchor, always my courage. My only reality."

"You left me." His voice was tender and accusing.

"It was for the best, Jericho. If I'd stayed, what would I have become? What would you?" Taking her hand from his, clutching the sheet, she sat up. Bracing against the bed, she looked around, remembering more than seeing the bold masculinity of the room. The neutral decor in ever-darkening tones, the perfect refuge for the quiet times of this worldly man who had been the boy she'd loved.

"You were a Rivers. With all the confidence the name commands, you knew who you were, and understood what you could be. I was a Delacroix. Until I left Belle Terre, I never understood I could be more than the outcast's brat. More than a girl with courtesan's blood in her veins. No better than a courtesan herself, in the eyes of Belle Terre's very proper society.

"Loving you was an impossible fairy tale that ended the night I was attacked. When the boys finished teaching me my place, one threatened rape. He was, as he saw it, only hurrying along the inevitable. Making clear to me what I could expect, what I would be, if I stayed in Belle Terre."

"Masked cowards," Jericho snarled. "They hurt you, and they took something precious from us. They didn't succeed in the rest, but their purpose was served." His face turned grim with the memory of the night he found her on a darkened street, fighting for her life. A young girl, his girl, clothes torn half away, a gang of boys, with stocking caps hiding their faces, circling her like a pack of wolves. "In the end, you believed them. Not in me."

"You were barely eighteen, Jericho. No matter what weight the Rivers name carried, no matter how strong and brave and honorable you were, you couldn't change the prejudices of an aristocratic Southern town." Maria stroked tangled sable locks from his forehead. "Darling, you still can't."

"That means you're leaving again."

"The story's finished. There's no more to be done here."

"What about this?" Catching her wrist, he drew her hand from his hair. "What does it mean?" A bangle threaded through a tiny gold band, then soldered into an unbroken circle, hugged her wrist. He hadn't spoken of it at the gala, or in the passion of the night. Now, as it glinted against the sheet, it took his breath away.

"A tribute." Maria answered. "To a memory I'll treasure

forever." A slight twist of her wrist and the matching band he wore lay as inexorably between them as the bangle. "Something beautiful that can only be a memory for both of us."

"If you should fall in love again? What happens then, Maria Elena Rivers?"

The name she'd carried in her heart for years brought tears to her eyes. Blinking them away, she shook her head. "I won't."

He wouldn't let it go at that. "And if I should?"

Pain clotted her throat. But because he deserved the life and love she couldn't offer, she gave him the only answer she could. "When that time comes, I won't stand in your way."

Jericho Rivers laughed. But only a fool would hear humor in the sound. "In half a lifetime our paths have crossed twice, with the same culmination. One wonders if that should tell us something."

"It does tell us something. We're star-crossed lovers, destined to love forever yet never meant to be. Belle Terre was the wrong place, our teen years were the wrong time."

"Do you ever wonder what might have happened if…?" Jericho's voice drifted into silence, leaving the rest unsaid.

As if she could wish the past away, she nodded. "If my father hadn't been that rare male of the Delacroix family? If he hadn't loved Belle Terre too much to leave it despite its archaic prejudices? If he'd never fallen in love with my mother, and she with him? If neither of them had ever picked up a liquor bottle? But most of all, if we'd met in college as strangers. Or in another life? Yes," she whispered softly. "I wonder. But—"

"But we didn't," he interrupted gently. "Instead we entered into a marriage that never began, yet never ends."

"Never began, never ends, but offers rare days like this."

Jericho smiled a real smile then, willing to leave the conundrum for another time. "So what do we do about it?"

"Well." Maria pretended to consider the possibilities. "The

day is hardly born, my bags are packed and my plane doesn't leave until long after six. All that's left to do is pick up the rental car from the museum parking lot.''

"It's also Sunday," Jericho contributed to the list of enticements. "My day off." A glance at a bedside clock told the time. "That leaves us more than twelve precious hours. Any idea how we could spend it, Mrs. Rivers?"

"One." Folding back the robe he wore, she slipped it from his shoulders and down his arms. "One very good idea, Sheriff Rivers." As silk fell away with his impatient shrug, she drew him to the bed, asking wickedly, "What else would star-crossed lovers do with such rare and wondrous hours as these?"

"Twelve hours? Sweetheart," Jericho groaned softly against her throat. "I don't think I have the stamina."

"Ah, my only love, you'll never know until you try."

His reply was a laugh and a kiss, as he began again a sweet, languid seduction. With tender restraint he caressed her, touching her face, stroking her hair, tracing the fan of her lashes as they lay against her cheeks. As if he'd never seen her or touched her before, he found the textures of her skin fascinating.

He was a man storing memories to last a lifetime, tracing the line and curve of her body, discovering once more his reasons for wanting her, for loving her. As she clung to him, her fleeting caresses driving him to the brink of distraction, he moved over her at last. For Jericho, the joining of his body with hers was as sweet as the first time, as poignant as if it were the last.

Then time and memory and reason ceased. There was only the passion of a man for a woman. And her need for him.

Like shadows cast against the fiery canvas of dawn he made love to her, and she to him. And when need was answered and passion spent, their passing brought peace and a quiet time to cherish.

Her head on his shoulder, his fingers woven through her

hair, they lay in sun glow and contented stillness. Long into
a drowsy silence, she stirred, her fingers trailed along his throat
and over his chest. With a hushed, wordless sound, she kissed
the heated curve of his throat, and sighed as she nestled against
him.

Beyond tall doors, a breeze stirred, rich leaves of summer
rustled in its promise of heat. A rising tide, tumbling sand and
shells, added another note in summer's waking song. In the
peace, trills of drowsy, childish laughter were borne on the
wind.

And somewhere in the distance, yet not too far, the cry of
a fitful baby rose and ebbed, then was silent.

Maria tensed, the lazy caress that moved lightly over the
contours of his throat and chest hesitated. She stared at sun-
washed leaves, but in her mind she saw darkness, not the last
of dawn. And glittering green fluttered against the backdrop
of an endless sky, with blue turned as black as the night.

As black as the night those long years ago. The unspoken
words sent a cold chill shuddering through her.

"Ah!" Her cry was torn from the depths of heartache. Her
fingers curled into tight fists. "Damn them! Damn them!"

Jericho made no move to hold her, no effort to stave off
the bitter, hurting rage. He knew where she'd gone. As he
waited for the brewing storm to break, he knew why.

He better than anyone understood she needed this. The rage,
the cleansing of silent hate. Only the unreal and inhuman
wouldn't. And Maria Elena Rivers was very real, very human.

"Were they there last night?"

Jericho only shook his head. She knew the answer as well
as he. Perhaps, in her subconscious, better.

"Was there one who offered me a glass of champagne? Or
asked me to dance? Dear God!" Bolting upright, she buried
her face in her hands. After a time that seemed forever, she
lifted her gaze to the light streaming through all doors. Shuddering, she whispered, "Did one of them touch me?

"I kept listening to voices, hoping I could recognize an

inflection, a tone, even a word. Once I was so sure. Then I didn't know." She paused again, reliving the past through the tarnished splendor of the evening.

Hearing her terror, hurting for it, Jericho waited silently for the rest. His wait was not long.

"I looked into the eyes of every man who approached me, searching for guilt, regret, remorse. Maybe concern or fear. Even gloating." Holding one hand before her, clasping it as if she held something abhorrent, she whispered, "For years I've tried to see a face hidden by the dark and the shadow of the tree—the face of the one boy whose mask I ripped off. But there's never anything.

"Then, tonight, there was. Only a sensation of recognition. No one person, nothing concrete, only an air of discomfort. The smell of fear. Then it was gone." A bitter laugh rattled in her throat. "I'm babbling, making no sense."

Drawing her hands through her hair, sweeping it from her face, she hardly noticed when it fell against her throat and cheeks again. "Maybe I wanted it so badly I imagined it. Maybe—" Stopping short, her head jerked in violent denial. "No."

Turning to him, not caring that the sheet slipped to her waist, she met his hurting gaze. "I'm not wrong. I don't know who, perhaps I never will, but one or all of them were there tonight."

Jericho drew a harsh, grating breath, desperate to hold her, to comfort her. But as much as he needed it, she needed the exorcism more. At last he said quietly, "You weren't wrong."

At the leap of surprise in her eyes, with two fingers he touched her cheek. "No, I don't know who they are, but I know the type. Few of our classmates who are living in Belle Terre would have missed the celebration, or the chance to see you."

"To discover what the tacky girl from the wrong family had become?" Maria wondered aloud. "Or testing my memory?"

"A little of both, I suspect." She'd walked among her tormentors head high, a calm, gallant smile for everyone. What had the men who'd been the boys who hurt her thought? Had they gloated? Cringed in fear of recognition? And, Jericho wondered, had any felt remorse? "We'll never know, sweetheart."

"Unless I remember." Taking his hand in hers, lacing her fingers through his, she recalled the gentleness of his touch, when others had been cruel. "But you don't think I ever will, do you?"

"I'm sorry." His thumb caressed the back of her hand, offering comfort for his doubt. "Not after such a long time."

"She would be eighteen, and a summer girl, if they'd let her live." Clinging to his hand and the stability of the present, in her mind she returned to a night so long ago. "The diner closed late, and I was hurrying to meet you on the beach. They were waiting, hidden in the shadows of the old oak. If I'd paid attention. If I'd been wary, she would have had a real birthday. Perhaps not the one we expected, but not the one they gave her."

"What could you have watched for, Maria Elena? What should you have been wary of?" Jericho refused to let her shoulder any part of the blame for the miscarriage of their child. "Belle Terre was the safest of places then. A sleepy town of unlocked doors and open windows. No one could have anticipated or predicted what happened.

"If anyone is to blame, it would be me. Until your shift was done, I should have waited for you at the diner, not on the beach."

"But you couldn't have known," Maria protested.

"No, I couldn't." Jericho made the point he intended as she rushed to defend him. "And neither could you."

Maria sank into silence, a somber look replacing the joy of the hours before. Gradually her frown softened. "I went by the cemetery, I saw the flowers. I thought you might forget."

"It isn't a date I'm likely to forget." Every year on a midsummer evening, he visited the secluded spot. There was only a tiny stone, its inscription simply Baby Girl. This was how Maria Elena had wanted it. To protect herself, or him? Or even the baby? He'd never had the chance to ask. She'd been too physically and mentally wounded to question.

Then, before he knew it, before she was truly recovered from the ordeal, she had gone, leaving behind the horror of Belle Terre. Leaving him. For these years he'd accepted this as what she wanted. And for years he'd left a small bouquet on the tiny pauper's grave.

"Thank you for that, Jericho." After a moment she added, "It's ironic, isn't it, that the museum would open and I would catch the assignment at exactly this time." Wearily, fatigue returning, her voice grew hoarse, her words an effort. "Or was it fate?"

Jericho didn't answer. Drawing her into his arms, he held her while they watched the morning sky. Too soon she would be leaving. The horror of a gentle seventeen-year-old girl was still too strong. Too vivid. He was losing her again. But until then, he would hold her and keep her safe.

He sensed the exact moment she drowsed. Her body grew heavy, the hand clasping his uncurled. Her breaths slowed to a measured rhythm. And he hoped that just for a while, she could rest.

Jericho had drifted into a somnolent state himself, when the jangling chime of his doorbell roused him. Slipping his arms from Maria Elena and covering her carefully, he pulled on his discarded slacks, then hurried to answer the summons.

"Court!" The deputy's normally spotless uniform was stained and smudged with soot. "What's wrong?"

"A problem at the museum."

"What sort of problem?"

"Just after dawn, a kid hot-wired a rental car in the museum parking lot. The culprit was the wannabe delinquent, Toby Parker."

"And?"

"The car blew him across the lot. Lucky for the kid it did. He's toasted around the edges and bruised, but he'll see his day in court. The rental burned to a twisted heap."

Startled, Jericho tried to think. "The museum isn't officially open. Why would a rental car be left in the lot?" Abruptly, like a knife in his heart, he understood. *Maria Elena.*

"We found enough of the tag to trace. That's how we know it was a rental. Ms. Delacroix's."

Jericho's head cleared, his response was coolly concise. "You've secured the area? Everyone knows what to do?"

"Yes, sir. No one touches anything until you get there."

"Good. Make sure nobody does. I'll be five minutes behind you." Closing the door after his deputy, Jericho stood with his hands on the heavy panels, his thoughts a morass of fear and worry. A light step and the rustle of cloth made him turn. Maria was there, in the bedroom doorway, a beautiful waif lost in the folds of his robe. The woman he loved, and must keep safe. "You heard?"

"I wondered what effect my homecoming might have on my old friends in Belle Terre." She was ashen, but calm. "Now we know."

"We don't know anything yet," Jericho contradicted. "Not even if it was a bomb. But whatever it was, it could have been gang related, targeting the kid who got singed. That it was your rental could be purely coincidence."

"Gangs in Belle Terre?" Maria made a doubting grimace.

"Damn right. Belle Terre isn't the sleepy, peaceful town you left eighteen years ago."

"Perhaps not," she conceded. "But you don't believe the bomb in my car was a coincidence any more than I believe it."

"I don't know what I believe," he admitted honestly. She was too astute not to recognize evasion. "We both know I can't make a judgment until the investigation is complete. For that reason I'll feel better when you're on the plane and out of reach."

"There's just one catch, Jericho."

His thoughts filled with the carnage she'd barely escaped, he looked at her, a questioning expression on his face.

"I won't be on that plane."

"Like hell you won't."

"Sorry, Sheriff." Oblivious of his robe puddling at her feet and flowing inches beyond her hands, she crossed her arms and leaned against the doorjamb. In a voice that was ominously pleasant, she declared, "Until this is resolved, I'm staying in Belle Terre."

"Dammit, Maria Elena..." He stopped as she slipped off his robe and let it fall at her feet. "What are you doing?"

"I'm getting dressed." Her comment was tossed over her shoulder as she walked away. "You should, too. Unless you plan to go in that particularly fetching, but unprofessional, state."

"Go where? What state?"

"To a bombing, darling. I've no choice but my gown. But, as sheriff, do you really want to go in tuxedo slacks, looking exactly like you just spent hours making love to your wife?"

"My wife?"

"Until you find someone else."

Jericho smiled hollowly. Maria Elena had just said the words he'd waited half his life to hear. At the time he least wanted to hear them. She shouldn't stay. He wouldn't let her if it was in his power to stop her. But even as he regretted her decision, he knew it was the decision he would have made.

To the world she was Maria Delacroix. To Jericho she was Maria Elena Rivers, a woman of extraordinary courage.

His wife.

"Until forever," he promised grimly. "If I can keep you safe."

Three

Maria Elena Delacroix Rivers moved like a cat. A very savvy cat who knew her way around the jungle. Any jungle. Even this one, and what it had become in an instant.

Her rental was a burned-out skeleton squatting in the nether regions of a long deserted parking lot. But, oddly, little around it showed more than the insidious signs of scorching from an intensely generated heat. Even the kid who'd decided to help himself to a joyride in the lone vehicle left unattended in the lot was okay. Just bruises, some burns, maybe a broken bone. A small price for a close call and a lesson, hopefully, well learned.

While rescue and police personnel dealt with the kid, Maria circled the car, studying it from every angle. As Maria studied the car, Jericho studied Maria.

Her work as a newscaster of no little fame also included quite a number of stints as a foreign correspondent. One such assignment had taken her to the Middle East. With her trusty microphone in hand, and her own personal camera never very far away, she'd put together riveting reports. With Pulitzer prize photographs thrown in for compassionate emphasis. Jericho remembered that many of her published photographs of that recent time portrayed scenes more than a little like this one.

"You've seen this before," he surmised as her circling inspection brought her close.

Maria's eyes narrowed, the piercing scrutiny of her gray, level gaze didn't alter, or turn from the car. "Almost," she answered softly. "But not quite."

A special bomb squad had flown in from Columbia 150 miles from Belle Terre. These experts in every known method of blowing a person, place, or thing to kingdom come, had studied every inch of the car, the parking lot, and the museum—with more to come later. Yet it was Maria who commanded Jericho's attention. Maria whose answers and opinions he sought. But this terse comment wasn't enough.

"Explain," Jericho said, softly. Very softly, but any who knew him would have recognized it as a tense command.

"It's different from the bombings I've seen and photographed." Maria turned now to look at him. "At first I thought he, whoever he might be, didn't know his stuff."

"And now?" Jericho had his own thoughts that had quickly grown into conviction. Now he wanted hers, with no other influence.

"Now I think he knew exactly what he was doing. The only thing he didn't take into consideration, and couldn't calculate, was our young car thief. Who just had the bad luck of being at the wrong place at the right time."

"Then you don't think the explosion occurred in tandem with ignition of the engine."

"Only as a coincidence. If it was truly in tandem at all." With splayed fingers, Maria combed the heavy wealth of her dark hair from her face and, again, didn't seem to notice that it fell back exactly as it had been. "I'm betting your experts have already found a timer. Probably as part of an incendiary device attached within the necessary proximity of the fuel tank.''

Jericho's head jerked once in admission, but he said nothing else. As intrigued as before, he watched and waited.

"This was meant to be a warning, Jericho." Maria didn't move this time as she raked the destroyed hull again with a narrowed stare. "Only a warning." She looked to him then, reading his concurring thoughts on his darkly grim face. "But as warnings go, it was worse than stupid."

Beyond the lift of a questioning brow barely visible beneath the tilt of his broad-brimmed hat, as sheriff, friend, and lover, he offered no opinion.

Maria crossed her arms beneath her breasts, mindful even in this lurid situation of the lingering tenderness left by the scrape of Jericho's beard and the sweet tug of his suckling. Curbing a sense of mourning for the exuberant innocence of those recent hours, her gaze scoured over the blackened steel one more time before returning to his. Her voice was soft, a little strained as it echoed the bitterness in her eyes. "Whoever he is, he's not only stupid, but a fool in the bargain."

"Stupid for this single, senseless act, because he answered the most critical question you asked yourself last night." Jericho spoke at last, quietly, with every trace of emotion carefully leached from his voice. "He was one of the patrons at the museum."

"A patron of the past of Belle Terre." The title seemed ludicrous given a less archaic past. A past that directly spawned this oblique attack. "A patron and a fool if he thinks that because I ran away once, I would again.

"Because things are different now," she said, almost to herself. "I'm not that frightened young girl from the wrong side of town anymore. And it's been a long time since I ran from anything."

Except me, Jericho wanted to say.

Only hours ago he would have given his soul to keep Maria in Belle Terre. But he knew that neither his soul nor his love was enough. Now that the gauntlet had been thrown and taken up, he wondered if it would mean her life if she stayed.

"Sheriff Rivers." Court Hamilton stood a pace away, a look of apology for intruding on an obviously intense conversation on his face. "Uncle…I'm sorry, sir. I meant, Captain Hamilton would like a word with you."

Yancey Hamilton, head of the state's special forces unit, was as much a gentleman as he was a professional. If he sent the deputy to interrupt what he would surely perceive as Jericho's interview of the intended victim, it was because he'd made an important discovery, or arrived at a pertinent opinion. Maybe one Maria Elena shouldn't hear. At least not just yet.

"Of course." Turning from his deputy to Maria, Jericho took her hand in both of his. "Beyond what further study the special investigators might need, there's nothing else to be done here. If you don't mind, I'll ask Deputy Hamilton to take you back to…"

"Back to the Inn at River Walk," Maria inserted for him. For reasons she didn't understand, and certainly couldn't explain, she didn't want to tarnish her memories of her night with Jericho with the shocking ugliness of the morning. "I have a room there. I was scheduled to check out this morning, but I doubt Eden Cade will object if I stay over for a bit longer."

Jericho would have felt better if she were tucked away in the safety of his own home. Or better yet, if she were miles removed from any threat of danger. But this was neither the time nor the place to discuss what he wanted for her.

"The Inn at River Walk, then." A frown channeled between his brows and deepened the lines at his eyes briefly before being chased away by a forced smile. Releasing her and stepping away, Jericho addressed his deputy. "Court, if you would, please escort Ms. Delacroix to her lodgings. Stay close, until Yancey and I have finished here and I'm free."

Deputy Hamilton snapped to attention crisply. "Yes, sir."

Maria realized then that he was probably one of Lady

Mary's students. As she had been, but not alongside her class-mates. The genteel but impoverished old lady, with her bright, birdlike eyes and manner, had spent her life teaching proper decorum and protocol to the children of the respected and affluent families of Belle Terre. Then there was Maria Elena Delacroix, the descendant of a long line of beautiful courte-sans.

But that was all part of the past. The distant past. Her past. Last night, for a little while, she'd hoped attitudes had changed, and who she'd been would be of little consequence.

Wrong? She'd never been more wrong. But she couldn't and wouldn't dwell on that now. Dismissing the intrusion of old memories, Maria focused her attention on Jericho.

He'd taken the time to dress in uniform. The austere lines of faultless dark khaki contributed even more to his air of extraordinary strength and quiet dedication. In black tie he'd been the epitome of the gracious Southern gentleman. In the dress of his profession, he became a cold-eyed, grim-faced veteran of the war against crime and disorder. Yet he delivered orders as if he were making a request. Orders surely more quickly obeyed for the manner in which they were given.

Maria's life in Belle Terre and afterward had made her cyn-ical. The eye of her camera saw with compassion. Her own eyes, her heart, her soul, did not. On the other hand, Jericho, she suspected, was that rare, indomitable professional in whom compassion and gentleness still lived and thrived, and ruled.

He'd proved that in the gentle way he'd made love to her, with no condemnation for her desertion, no bitterness for the lost years. What sort of man was this? Maria wondered as she asked, "You'll call me when you have a definitive report?"

Beyond taking her hand, Jericho hadn't touched her since they'd arrived at the parking lot. He'd offered no explanation for the fact that they'd arrived together. With one steady, chal-lenging look from him, no one dared comment that Maria still wore the gown of flowing gold, sparkling brighter in the morn-ing sun than it had in the muted light of the museum. With his own circumspect behavior and the dare in his unflinching stare, he'd protected her from any threat of gossip. Now or later. For she knew intuitively, and from the respect shown by Jericho's men, there would be no scandalized or secret lecherous whispers behind shielding hands.

Now, with the gentle cupping of his palm against her cheek, Jericho broke his own unspoken rule of discretion. "I promise. But I'll do better than call, Maria Elena. I'll drop by the inn when we've done all we can here."

Maria wanted to cover his hand with her own, keeping his touch. More than that, she wanted to turn her mouth into his palm and with her lips trace the hard, calloused strength. She wanted to watch his eyes as she touched her tongue to that dark, gentle hollow the calluses protected. As he had protected her when she was seventeen.

As he would protect her now.

As if he read her thoughts, he leaned close, his breath a warm caress against her cheek. "Go along with young Court, love. There's nothing more to fear. For now."

"I know." She did stroke his hand then, in gratitude. She did brush her lips over the pad of his thumb, briefly. Too briefly. But with it a thunderbolt of desire struck as ungoverned and as stunning as if it were the first time.

For Jericho, too, she realized, for his gray gaze darkened and his breath stuttered. But it was only a heartbeat before his teeth clamped together with such force a muscle flickered like the lightning of this sensual, sexual storm.

"Go," he managed hoarsely. His right hand, with the burnished gold band gleaming, fell from the soft allure of her lips. "I'll be with you as soon as I can."

Maria only nodded, her eyes and her heart too full of her need for him to speak. With one smoldering look, she turned. Taking the arm Deputy Hamilton gallantly extended, like a queen she glided through the gathering crowd, oblivious of the rapt gazes of Jericho's trusted friends and fascinated colleagues.

The sun was almost gone when Jericho climbed the steps that would lead to the entry of River Walk. He'd wakened with the sun and Maria...now he would end a long, grueling day with them. He'd been longer at the museum than he expected. Worse, this first and crucial investigation had yielded far less than he hoped.

The only conclusion anyone set forth with any confidence was that the person, or persons, who constructed the simple device then, on a gamble, set it for an hour it would be unlikely anyone would be near, meant no harm to anyone.

"This time," Jericho muttered, as he opened the massive leaded glass door leading to the reception room of the inn.

This time. But what about the next? Or the next? Having failed in scaring Maria away, would this frantically desperate man try again? And again, if he must?

Jericho had wanted Maria to stay. More than anything in all his life, he'd *needed* her to stay, to build a life with him. Now, torn and hurt by the logic, he knew she must go.

"Jericho?" Eden Cade paused in the doorway of the reception room, a covered tray in her hands. Her welcoming smile was worried. "We'd almost given up on you for dinner."

"Tonight? Dinner with you and Adams?" Jericho searched his mind, wondering if he'd forgotten an invitation. But surely he hadn't—no one ever passed up a chance for a meal at the Inn at River Walk. Then, again, maybe he had forgotten. Since he'd learned Maria would be covering the opening at the museum for her network, he'd thought of nothing else.

"Heavens, no," Eden exclaimed. "Adams isn't here." With an amused and glowing glance at the slight protrusion of her stomach, she laughed aloud. "He's been rushing around for a week now, taking care of anything and everything he thinks might need his attention before the baby comes."

"So soon?" Eden was carrying small, but that small? Jericho frowned, wondering if he'd miscounted, or mixed up the date Adams had announced for the birth of his child.

Eden laughed again, and Jericho had never seen this always

beautiful woman so beautiful. "Of course not. But tell that to Adams. He plans to have a clean slate for the next three months so he can join with Cullen in driving me crazy. In fact, if either my husband or my chief steward saw this tray in my hand, both would very likely suffer from a dire case of apoplexy."

Jericho grinned. He could easily believe it of both men. Adams Cade, inventor and businessman par excellence, had been a friend all his life. But when Adams returned to Belle Terre and married Eden, all his successes paled in comparison. It was the same with Cullen. When he'd come with Eden to Belle Terre, no one expected the massive islander to be happy here. But soon it was obvious that the native of the Marquesas Islands had transferred his undying loyalty from Nicholas Claibourne and the islands to Eden, Nicholas's widow. Loyalty that remained unswerving in her marriage to Adams, her first and true and everlasting love.

Any other time, Jericho would have chuckled at the idea of Cullen, the only man he knew who was nearly as big as he, acting the lady's maid for a gloriously pregnant Eden Cade. But now, his mind was too full of Maria. Too full, and too worried even to celebrate the joy and wonder of the coming birth of a child the most revered medical minds of the world had believed could never be conceived.

"Forgive me, Eden." Jericho felt a sudden twinge for his neglectful preoccupation. "Let me take that."

"Surely." Eden relinquished the tray graciously. "And thank you, Jericho."

"Where would you like me to take it?"

"Actually, your arrival was perfectly timed." With a hand at his shoulder, she led him to the small elevator Adams had just installed. "I was taking the tray to the third floor."

"The top?" Once Eden had kept her apartment on the top floor. To afford both herself and the guests of the inn more privacy. But after their marriage, she and Adams had chosen to live in the river cottage, a secluded and private residence on the grounds of River Walk. "I thought…"

"That Adams and I live in the cottage?" Eden paused before the elevator, pressed a small button and, by a newly acquired habit, folded her arms protectively over her stomach. "We do."

The door of the elevator slid open without a sound. It was typical of Adams that it would work perfectly and unobtrusively. When, with gentlemanly courtesy, Jericho waited for Eden to precede him, she shook her head. "I'm not going."

"No?"

With another shake of her head, her smile widened. "I was going to keep Maria Elena company for a bit. But now that you're here, she won't need my company. Cullen's with her now. He took the liberty of bullying poor Court Hamilton into agreeing to watch the grounds. But I imagine Maria's self-appointed guardian will relinquish his post while you're with her."

"Cullen's watching over Maria Elena, on the third floor?"

"Of course. It was his idea that Maria should move to the third floor. Then he insisted that he should keep watch over her until we know more about the explosion. It was also his idea that the chef should prepare a cold dinner for two—for when you managed to get away. So." Eden stepped back from the door. With a wave and a twinkle in her eyes, she murmured, "Enjoy, old friend. Be as happy tonight as you can."

The elevator moved soundlessly and quickly, then stopped without a jolt. The door slid open as silently. Cullen was there in the foyer, far bigger than the chair that surely creaked under his weight. A book on Southern gardening lay open on his knees, and a pair of fragile half glasses perched haphazardly on his broad nose.

A smile lit the islander's face when he recognized Maria's visitor. As a blunt finger slanted a warning for quiet across finely shaped lips, Jericho knew that fatigue and the stress of the day had likely demanded its due.

"Maria Elena's sleeping?"

A tilt of his head was Cullen's only response.

"Then I'll watch over her now, Cullen. Until she wakes."

Rising from his chair, with his gardening book folded under his arm, the islander opened the door that would lead to the suite where Maria had been kept safe. Jericho stepped through and turned, the tray still in his hands. "Thank you, Cullen, for everything."

Cullen smiled and stepped into the elevator. With his huge hand he kept the door ajar. "Keeping watch was my pleasure, Sheriff. Miss Delacroix reminds me of Miss Eden." His words were a low rumble, meant only for Jericho. "A brave woman, but deeply hurt by life, and sad."

"Her name is Rivers, Cullen. Maria Elena Rivers. We were married eighteen years ago." Jericho should have been surprised that he'd said the words. He wasn't. But the last sin that could be laid at Cullen's door was gossip. The man held his confidences as determinedly as a clam.

The islander's smile gleamed brighter, with no trace of surprise. "Then, now that you're here, perhaps Mrs. Rivers's sadness will ease. As it did for Miss Eden when Adams came home to her."

Cullen took his hand away. The door began to close. "Have a good night, sir. Rest assured I won't be far away."

Jericho had no chance to acknowledge the islander's assurance, but he knew Cullen well enough to know he didn't expect a response. Instead he closed the door, set the supper tray on the nearest table, and went in search of Maria.

The suite was typically Eden. Large rooms, minimally but elegantly appointed. And, of course, there were flowers. In every alcove there was whatever arrangement the space and design could accommodate. Yet even in that, Eden's taste and preference erred on the side of pleasing rather than overwhelming. But that there were flowers was the important factor.

Maria Elena loved flowers. Jericho liked to think their little girl would have loved them as well.

The bedroom was darkened by closed shutters. The massive bed, lying in disarray, was empty. His seeking gaze followed a muted beam of light to Maria.

She stood before a narrow door, its shutter half open, letting the light of the setting sun spill through it. Maria wore a gown and a robe of silk that gleamed in the little light like a pale emerald. Her arms were crossed beneath her breasts, the tousled mass of her hair tumbled against her cheek as she stared down on the gardens of River Walk.

"Have you considered how ironic it is, after all these years, and all that's happened, that I'm here, Jericho?"

Jericho had paused where he was. He had no idea how she knew she wasn't alone, or even who waited in the doorway. Perhaps the cadence of his quiet step? A familiar scent? The sixth sense of lovers with its knowing recognition?

"Do you mean here in Belle Terre? Here at River Walk? Or on Fancy Row?" he asked softly, though he was sure he knew.

"Fancy Row—that says it all, doesn't it?" She turned to him then, and he saw that if she'd slept, it hadn't been restful. "Fancy for the sort of women who lived here. The mistresses of wealthy planters who kept them in luxury and dressed them like queens, yet wouldn't recognize either the women or the children they bore them. Row, because even these homes among the finest in the city didn't deserve the respect of having a street."

"What you say *was* true, but no more," he countered as she paced toward him, the gown skimming her knees, the robe swaying over her unbound breasts. "Times change, Maria Elena. So do people."

"Do they?" In a familiar gesture, she threaded her fingers through her hair, combing it back from her face. Before her hand had moved completely away, the dark strands were falling again in a veil over her cheek. "There are those who will think it's fitting that I'm staying here. The child of a Delacroix, living on the street where the Delacroix courtesans plied their sinful trade.''

''Legend has it the Delacroix were the most beautiful, most accomplished women in the low country. A prize for one man to claim. Even to duel for, Maria Elena. Yet you paint them as whores, little better than streetwalkers going from man to man.''

''Not from man to man,'' Maria corrected bitterly. ''To the highest bidder.''

''To one man, to whom each was faithful,'' he reminded.

''For whom they bore illegitimate children. Always to be known as Delacroix, never by their father's name.''

''Keeping a mistress, being a mistress, was an accepted practice of the time, my love. But nothing to do with you.'' He would have reached out to take her in his arms, but he knew that in this mood, she would reject him.

''You're wrong, Jericho. It has everything to do with me. I'm a Delacroix, a reminder of an accepted but unsavory custom. In Belle Terre, nothing is ever forgotten. Why else did I lose our child?''

''They were just boys, Maria Elena. Certainly misguided, certainly cruel. But still boys. Foolish, thoughtless boys.''

''And bigots,'' Maria snapped. With her arms clutched ever more tightly about her, she turned her back on him. ''Like all the good citizens of Belle Terre.''

Jericho hadn't bothered to change out of his uniform, but his broad-brimmed hat had been left downstairs. Now, in frustration, he scrubbed a hand over his eyes and his forehead, dislodging a dark lock that drifted over his temple. Letting his hand fall away in a loosely curled fist, he asked softly, ''Does that sweeping opinion include me? Or Eden? How about Adams and his brothers? Or Lady Mary? Have you forgotten she was kind to you?''

Her back was still turned to him. When her tirade began,

her shoulders had been stiffly erect. Now they curled as if she flinched from the acrimony of her bitter judgment.

"Does it, Maria Elena? Are we all intolerant snobs, simply because we aren't all descendants of the Delacroix beauties? Have you forgotten that your lost summer girl was my little girl and my loss, as well?"

"I...no." Keeping her back to him, she shook her head slowly, then fell silent to stand mutely in sunset.

In the broken denial, Jericho heard the threat of tears. He had to go to her then. Nothing on earth could have stopped him from holding her. Not even fear of rejection. Nor rejection itself.

Yet when he gathered her in his embrace, she turned to him, her arms hard about him, her mouth lifting greedily to his.

With Maria the initiator and the leader, their kiss was long and wild and deep. Her teeth nipped at his lips, but only for her tongue to soothe the hurt. Her hands slipped between the crush of their bodies to slide over his chest, his throat. Circling to his nape, her fingers tangled in the dark hair brushing his collar, but only to drag him fiercely down to her. She couldn't get him close enough. The teasing caress of probing, twining tongues wasn't deep enough, hard enough.

"More," she muttered as she released the clutch of his hair, and turned her attention to the buttons of his shirt. "I want to feel you. I want the touch of your skin on mine. I want your hands on me. I want you. Only and forever, you."

"No, my love. No." He caught her hands, pinning them between the unyielding musculature of his chest and the enticing softness of her breasts. "I'm sooty. I stink of smoke and grease."

"You're Jericho. That's all that matters." As she whispered the last, she leaned to kiss their joined hands. Then, slowly, her head lifted and she rose on tiptoe to touch her lips to the pulse that fluttered like a captured bird at the hollow of his throat. The touch of her tongue sent the heat of an inferno racing from his throat to pool hot and heavy in his groin.

Then, she lifted her head to let her gaze reach into his. In the half light of twilight in an ever-darkening room, he saw that her eyes of shimmering silver were filled with fear. Not fear of dying, but of never having truly lived.

She wanted him now, as an affirmation of life. In her eyes he saw grief for the little life they'd lost, for the life they'd never had together, even the life they might never have. But this moment was theirs. No one and nothing could take it from them.

"Yes." He answered the question she hadn't asked, except with her eyes. "Yes."

In a single motion he nearly ripped her nightclothes from her body. Before the emerald silk could pool at her feet, he swept her into his arms to stalk the length of the room. Laying her gently on the bed, he straightened to tear away his own clothes.

She watched him. As buttons ripped from their moorings, her gaze raked over every inch of exposed flesh. Next his belt was flung away. The snap at the waist of his trousers opened, the zipper growled. As if by magic, trousers and boots and every shred of clothing were gone from him.

He towered over her, all six and a half manly feet of Jericho Rivers. So handsome, so aroused, so ready. He wanted her. He needed her more than he'd ever wanted, ever needed, before. Yet with all the strength and reason he possessed, he waited.

Maria understood. She must set the pace. Allowing herself one last worshiping look, she opened her arms, whispering, "Make me feel real, Jericho. Teach me to be glad I'm alive."

Then he came down to her. There was no seduction, no foreplay. The time for that had passed. Maria Elena wanted what he wanted. She needed what he needed—his body joining with hers, stroking hers, hard, fast, deep. Over and over again until their bodies lifted and arched seeking even more.

He didn't think of hurting her. He didn't feel her nails tearing across his shoulders and down his chest. He only heard her whisper *yes,* and *yes,* and *yes,* as he gathered her wrists in his hands and pinned them over her head.

With her hands held captive as she arched to meet the power of his thrust, he bent to kiss her breast. Yet despite their madness, his suckling was as gentle as their mating was fierce.

Her breasts were fragrant from the bath oils for which the Inn at River Walk was famous. Their flavor gathered in his lungs, on his skin, and his tongue. Flavors and scents that banished the acrid memory of explosives and fire. There was no car, no young thief, no burned hulk. Only a man and a woman. Only Jericho and Maria Elena.

When he bent to suckle for the last time, he felt the first beginning shudders clasping him. Then she was struggling to free her hands, but only to draw his mouth to hers. Only to mate with him with lips and tongue, as she had with soul and body.

This had begun out of unfathomed need. As coupling in animal heat. As lust. As sex. But it was cleansing passion and abiding love that drew them to its splendid conclusion.

As she wrapped him in that splendor, giving of herself even as she took from him, she was his friend, the center of his universe. His reason for living.

The woman he loved.

His wife.

Four

Jericho woke with the dawn, out of habit and custom. As he had before, he sat by Maria's bed watching her sleep, while memories swirled through his mind. Not just memories of the night, but of their years as children and teens in Belle Terre.

In the pall of those long-ago memories, a smile bearing no trace of humor or joy twisted his lips and turned his eyes to seething pits. He'd known Maria Elena Delacroix almost all his life. And loved her passionately and hopelessly for nineteen of those years. Sometimes, as now, he suspected he had loved her even longer.

During the night, they'd roused, showered together and made love again. Now, as she slept, with her drying hair rippling over the pillow, in spite of telltale marks of intemperate passion, it was the innocence of a frightened girl he saw. An exquisite young girl eager to be accepted, eager to be liked.

But that was before she truly understood what it meant to be a Delacroix. Especially in Belle Terre. Before she discovered she would never be forgiven for the perceived sins of any number of distant grandmothers, aunts, and cousins. Before she realized that being smarter and more beautiful than the other girls of Belle Terre Academy, *and* a Delacroix, was an unforgivable combination.

The first time he'd seen her, she was a scrawny little thing, with changeable gray eyes too big for her face, and a wealth of shiny hair as black as sin. She was just ten, a brand-new student at the academy. More than a little lost and confused, and totally overwhelmed by the affluence of her new surroundings. He was eleven, almost twelve, a veteran of six years at the private academy.

While she was unbelievably tiny, he was already the biggest kid his side of high school. So, on her first day, when she'd fumbled unfamiliarly with her locker, spilling her new books all over the hall, it seemed natural that he would pick them up, then offer to carry them as he showed her to her first class.

That was the beginning of "Jericho and Maria." Out of a simple courtesy that was second nature to a tenderhearted boy, grew a unique friendship that forged a lasting bond.

There were repercussions from the beginning. Some vicious teasing, hate-filled remarks. Later, he understood that his classmates were parroting parental attitudes. A few of the boys scoffed at him for liking any girl. But especially the new girl, whom everyone seemed to be certain shouldn't be attending the academy at all.

But even at eleven, almost twelve, Jericho had liked her smile. He liked the serious gaze that always seemed to find him, no matter where he was or what he was doing. He liked pretty Maria and her eyes and her smile more than he hated the teasing.

He knew she was different from the other girls. He knew there was something more than the unspoken class system of the proud Southern town that set her apart. But Jericho's mother was a Yankee and a maverick, the only black mark against the most aristocratic Rivers name. In her own words, Leah Rivers didn't give "a cup of tea in hell" for the townfolk's preoccupation with whose father was who and had what. She didn't care whose long-lost ancestor had signed what document or led what cavalry charge where. She found the deadly serious celebration of family connections and claim of old money foolish and intolerably arrogant.

In an inexplicable peculiarity of the cliquish Southern town, this very disdain made Leah Rivers one of Belle Terre's most respected women. Because she practiced her beliefs, judging people by their own accomplishments, Jericho never understood the parroted slurs. It was a classmate who enlightened him, whispering behind a shielding hand a tale of half truths and embellished lies of what the Delacroix women had been nearly a century before.

It was then he'd visited his grandmother. His father's mother, *Grandmère* Rivers, as she preferred to be addressed. More than an equal and a match for her daughter-in-law in brutal frankness, this proud and patrician old lady was, nevertheless, the revered ruler of society in Belle Terre. But, as she warned him in the course of their talk, even she couldn't control the misguided cruelties and injustices of prejudice.

He was thirteen the day of their talk, and admittedly naive. But before she was through, he understood the facts, the myths, the foibles, and the pain of the wealthy Southern gentleman's penchant for keeping a mistress and even a second family. He understood that once it had been a common, expected social institution.

Grandmère had saved the Delacroix women for last. With her back ramrod straight and her chin tilted, she'd spoken of a family of daughters. Girls of lesser means, noticed first for their comeliness, then their innate soft-spoken gentility. Traits that became consistent as their name and beauty became legend.

They were few, their intelligence and style always unique. Making their liaisons the most sought after, bringing the highest prices on the bidders's market. Eventually it became an accepted fact that the prettiest Delacroix girlchild would be groomed from birth to be a courtesan. Yet, only if the young woman accepted the terms of the bidder. If she accepted, the relationship would be permanent.

"It was rare, almost unheard of, that a Delacroix ever had more than one lover," Grandmère emphasized. "Beyond his wife, neither would her patron.

"Not a good practice, Jericho." Almost too softly to be heard, she added, "But not the worst that could have happened for all who were involved either."

There was more, Jericho remembered. Over lemonade and Grandmère's special sugar cookies, she explained many customs of the past. Some good. Some bad. Some a mix of both. Some silly. Some confusing. Some surprising.

But the greatest shock of all was learning that his own grandfather, in the course of a life cut short, had kept a mistress.

"Ah, yes," Grandmère assured him. "She was a pretty little thing. Not big and horsey as I. Your grandfather kept her in exquisite style for years. With my blessing. But, thank God, there were no children."

Faded eyes that once had been the exact color of his own, searched his face. "Rest assured, Jericho, my sweet boy, you have no secret uncles, or aunts, or cousins strolling the streets of Belle Terre. Your grandfather might have been a bounder, he might have thrown away half a fortune, his excesses might have led to an early death, but, in the little he did right, a second family was not an added complication."

"Didn't you care, Grandmère?"

He could still remember how his voice trembled when he thought of how the man who had never been more to him than a portrait over the dining room mantle and a name on a grave-stone must have hurt this grand and beloved lady.

But when she'd glimpsed his sickened expression, Letitia Rivers had taken his face between her pale beringed hands, saying the words he had never forgotten.

"Jericho, my sweet child, your not-so-dear departed grandfather is proof one's station in life does not guarantee a good and wise, or even a kind, person. That you must always understand.

"But most important, you must know and believe that your grandfather's having kept a mistress doesn't make you a bad person. No more that the Delacroix women having been mistresses makes your little friend anything but what she is—a sweet, beautiful, and intelligent child."

"Then I should keep on being her friend, Grand-mère?" he asked, too preoccupied by all she'd told him to wonder how at seventy-two Letitia Rivers could know that Maria Elena was sweet, beautiful, intelligent, or anything at all.

When he remembered later, he'd shrugged it off. After all, in his eyes, Grandmère Rivers, grand dame of Belle Terre society, knew everything.

She'd peered at him over the lorgnette she stubbornly preferred to glasses. As if she'd assessed his courage and approved, at last, she nodded. "Of course you should."

"Good," he replied as he leaned to kiss her wrinkled cheek, "'cause I intended to all along."

Grandmère Rivers chuckled, delighted with him. As he left the room, she called after him, "Bring little Miss Delacroix by to see me one day. We'll have lemonade and sugar cookies."

"I will," he promised.

But, somehow, he never had.

The years had flown by too fast. As *Grandmère* said he should, he remained Maria's steadfast friend, and she, his. Sometimes against intolerable odds.

Friendship grew stronger and deepened, turning into an unexpected sexual attraction, then love. Together, in the unguarded heat of passion, they'd made a baby, then married, keeping both secret while they considered what to do next.

The decision was taken from them by the brutal, unprovoked attack. In the beat of a wounded heart, the baby was gone.

Shortly afterward, so was Maria Elena.

Leaving Jericho to go on with his life, with only a gold band to remind him of all he'd lost.

"But you're here now," he whispered. "And, in spite of how much I want you, I must convince you to go."

Brushing a dark tendril from her face, he stroked her cheek. Then, linking his fingers through hers and lifting them to his kiss, he rested his forehead on their joined hands.

He didn't know how long he sat there, his mind a morass of worry for Maria, and guilt for not having anticipated trouble. Perhaps a few minutes had passed, perhaps only seconds, when her clasp tightened and she whispered his name.

"Hello, sleepyhead." He tried to keep his tone light, but when a frown flitted across her face, he knew he'd failed.

Rising on one elbow, as she took her hand from his, in a slow and continuous caress she brushed back his hair and traced the line of his throat. "You look so troubled." Resting her palm over his bare chest, measuring the beat of his strong, brave heart, she asked, softly, "Are you angry with me?"

"Angry?" Sliding her palm from his chest to his lips, he kissed the dark, damp hollow, and breathed in the scent of her. "Why should I be angry with you, love?"

"For coming back into your life." Her gaze followed the

pad of her thumb as she drew it across his lower lip, tugging at it like a kiss. "For interrupting your love life, and for bringing trouble to your peaceful little city."

"Are you back in my life, Maria Elena?" In spite of his efforts, Jericho's voice was strained. "Or was this just a one night stand along the way in your travels?"

"Two nights," Maria corrected lightly, belying the flicker of hurt that crossed her face as her hand drifted to the bed. "So, should we call this an affair along the way in my travels?"

Jericho drew back, his arms crossed over his chest, his eyes narrowed. "Suppose you tell me, Maria Elena. Eighteen years is a long time between lovers." Then softly, "Or is it?"

Maria couldn't listen to any more. Not when she still lay in the bed where he'd made love to her. Tossing back the covers, she bolted away from Jericho and the bed. Catching up her robe from the floor where he'd discarded it in haste, she slipped into it. Crossing to the tall windows she threw open the shutters. Sunlight streamed in, warming the silk of her robe. Yet even with the robe and the light, she felt exposed and cold.

Staring down on the garden, Maria struggled to think, to find a reason for his attitude. Yesterday had been draining and stressful. It would've been natural for Jericho to be irritable then. But it made no sense now when the night they shared... "No."

"What does that mean?" Jericho questioned. He'd left his place by the bed. Now he stood only a pace behind her. "No, eighteen years isn't a long time. Or no..."

Maria whirled to face him, her hair flying like a dark mist in sunbeams. "It means, no, I'm not going to let you do this."

"This?" A dark brow lifted over a gray gaze she saw was bleak and hurting.

When he'd risen from the bed they'd shared, he'd drawn on his trousers and no more. As he stood barefoot, bare chested, in need of a shave, and utterly magnificent, Maria's rush of hurt and anger ebbed, but not her determination. "I won't let you create a rift between us to drive me away.

"I'll answer any question you want to ask about my lovers through the years. But I won't quarrel with you, Jericho. And I won't leave Belle Terre."

"Dammit, Maria Elena!" An agitated palm cupped the back of his neck. A holdover she remembered from his teenage years, and a sure sign of tension.

"That is what this is all about, isn't it?" Maria advanced a step, which brought her close enough to prod his chest with one finger. "You want me to leave Belle Terre, don't you? You want it desperately enough that you would deliberately destroy what we've shared. If it will accomplish your purpose."

A nail like a rapier prodded his hard, muscular chest again. "Forget it, buster."

Catching her hand, he plastered it against his chest, hard. "Dammit, Maria Elena, you aren't thinking straight. You don't belong here, especially not now."

"First of all, my name isn't 'Dammit Maria'. Second, you're wrong. For the first time in eighteen years I *am* thinking straight. This is exactly where I belong. It's where I've always belonged."

With her hand still caught within his grasp, her nails still scratched easily over his chest, catching the tip of a brown, flat nipple. Masking her delight when his breath caught in his throat and he couldn't quite restrain a small shudder, she moved in for the *coupe de vérité*. "Third, addressing your questions of lovers. Yes, in eighteen years I've had many. Hundreds. If we do the math, maybe it will figure out to thousands."

"I don't want…"

"You don't want to hear it? Tough." Maria cut him off. "You asked the question, Mr. Sheriff Jericho Rivers, you're going to know who my lovers were. You're going to hear how they looked, and how they made me feel."

Maria could've sworn his handsome, weathered face paled, as his seething glare strafed over her, devouring her. As if seeing her as another lover might. Imagining another lover touching her.

As her body responded to the heated, possessive look, she caught back an unsteady sigh and launched into her answer. "My legion of lovers are all of a type. All are kind. Gentle. All dark, stronger than the strongest oak, and taller than the sky. They all have eyes as silvery gray as a stormy sea. And they come to me in the night, wherever I am. Africa. Egypt, China, Russia. Belle Terre.

"They come to me only in my wishes and my dreams." Her free hand trailed over his jaw, her fingertips lingered at his mouth. "Because all my lovers are you, Jericho. Wherever I am, wherever I go, only you."

"Ah, damn..." This time Jericho's groaned curse was interrupted by a kiss. His own, as he hauled her hard against him, nearly crushing her ribs in shame, in relief, and desperate need. Maria was on tiptoe, surging to meet him as he bent from his great height. Lips and tongue dueled and fought, then softened and caressed, as the turbulent, desperate edge that always colored the first of their lovemaking calmed.

He'd lifted her off her toes, soothing her sweet, ravaged mouth with his, when he raised his head from her and released her with an ironic reluctance. "A thousand lovers?" he muttered. "Little wanton. What am I going to do with you?"

"I have an idea." The rapier nail skimmed down his chest to hover at the band of his trousers. "But since it's Monday and a workday, and since you surely don't want to go to work in a sooty uniform, I suppose my idea will have to wait."

"I have an hour yet." Burying his fingers in her hair, he drew her back to him. Resting his head on hers, he muttered, "An hour to make sure you're safe."

"With Cullen close by, I don't think either of us has anything to worry about."

"If you insist on staying, I want you in my home," he said,

still surprised because it hadn't occurred to him she wouldn't prefer his place over the busy inn.

"No." Maria spoke softly, but the ring of determination was in the single word. "I think that what's between us needs to be resolved before we live together. It's obvious the attraction is still all-consuming. But the fact remains that it's been eighteen years. We're different people now. Until we know those different people better, we shouldn't make a commitment of any sort."

"It wouldn't have to be a commitment, Maria Elena. I would never hold you to anything you don't want."

"Does either of us know what we want?" she asked quietly. "Beyond friendship and good sex?"

"I think I do." What Jericho wanted now was what he'd always wanted—Maria in his life, making a life with him. A tiny, living, breathing life.

"You *think*," she repeated with emphasis.

"Scratch that, it was just a figure of speech." Tilting her chin, he brushed her lips with his. "I know what I want. I've always known. Since the day you told me you were having my child."

Tears gathered in her eyes, but she ducked her head and blinked them away. In a ragged voice she murmured, "That's all the more reason to be sure."

"You won't change your mind? You won't come home with me?"

Heaven help her, there was nothing Maria wanted more. Nothing she'd ever in all her life wanted more. But so much had stood in their way the first time, so much had gone wrong, she couldn't risk her heart so naively again. She couldn't endure another tragic loss. And that's what having to leave Jericho a second time would be, a tragedy. One she wouldn't survive.

The shake of her head was sorrowful, regretful. "Not yet, Jericho. It's too soon. There are too many factors clouding the issue. But that doesn't mean we can't see each other. Spend long chunks of time together.''

"Sleep together." Jericho added to the list. "Make love together. And it would be love, Maria Elena." Drawing the back of his hand over the soft underside of her chin, he asked hoarsely, "Would you deny us that, my love? Could you?"

"How could I? All you have to do is touch me." She spoke the truth almost desperately. "The last two days have proven that."

It was the same with Jericho. He'd been only half a person for nearly half his life. But he hadn't known it until Maria Elena came back into his life, touching his soul, healing his heart.

"Tonight, then?" he asked gently. "We could have dinner in the dining room here." With his massive hand, he ruffled her hair, loving the feel of it as it slipped like burnished, black silk between his fingers. "Then..."

"Then we could come back up here." Suddenly she laughed a breathless laugh. "Listen to us. We've only just begun, but we already sound like an old married couple, finishing each other's sentences."

"I like the way you finish my sentences. If there was time, I'd show you just how much I like it." Tearing his fascinated gaze from her lovely, changeable eyes, and glancing at his watch, Jericho frowned. "Right now, I'm afraid time is something we don't have."

"So." Locking her arms at his waist, leaning into him, Maria sighed. Then, tilting her head, she smiled up at him. "I gather that means that each of us must dress and get on with our day."

"Maria Elena." Framing her face between his hands, abruptly solemn, he stared down into the gray gaze, reflecting bewitching hints of her emerald robe. "I realize you're no stranger to danger. But for the most part, only as an observer. This is different. This time you could be the target."

"Why are you telling me this now, Jericho?"

"Because there are certain precautions I have to put into place. Certain restrictions you have to observe. Will you?"

She saw then how deep his concern went. How frightened he was for her. Jericho had always been the biggest, the strongest, the bravest. She'd only seen him frightened once before. And that one time had been for her, and their baby.

"I'll do anything you say," Maria agreed, unable to deny him that much. "Anything except leave."

Jericho's lips quirked in a grimace, but he didn't argue as he led her to a chair. Once she was seated, he gathered the lapels of her robe closer about her, muttering, "Your bare legs are distraction enough without adding more."

"Sorry," she murmured, assuming a prim and proper posture that only made Jericho want to haul her into his arms and his lap, to protect her and love her.

Instead, he sat across from her, his big frame dwarfing the chair, as he explained in detail what precautions and safeguards he would set in motion. Next, just as seriously, he outlined the rules and regulations, and the cooperation he expected from Maria.

By the time he'd slipped into his shirt and shoes and made a stab at controlling his hair, he'd left no detail unaddressed or unplanned. "Come." Extending his hand to her, he said, "Walk me to the door, Maria Elena."

Hand in hand they crossed the spacious room. He in the sooty uniform, a grim reminder of the morning before. She in her carefully and primly arranged robe. Pausing, with thumb and forefinger at her chin, Jericho tilted her face and her gaze to his. "I'm sorry."

"For what?" Maria was truly perplexed.

"For snarling like an ill-tempered beast." Stroking away the frown lines at her forehead, he explained, "You were right. It wasn't a conscious act or plan, but I realize now that I was trying to drive you away. Not because I don't want you. I think I've made it indelibly clear that I do. That I always will.

"If I could have my way in this, I would still want you to leave. But only until we resolve this."

"Which could be never, Jericho." Her look was level and determined. "I ran once, and lost more than I knew. I'm older now, and wiser. I won't run again."

"You'll be careful?" He insisted, as much as asked. "Do exactly as I've said? Remember, if you need anything, or if anything out of the ordinary happens, Cullen and Court will be close."

"Yes, sir." A smile accompanied her promise.

The smile that was lost on Jericho as he gathered her in his arms, muttering into her hair. "God help me, I don't want to leave you. Not even for a minute."

"But you have a job to do, and a city to protect." Rising to her tallest as she brought his head down to hers, on a kiss she promised, "When you finish, I'll be waiting."

Jericho left without another word, or another touch. By the time he reached the street, his face was grave. He had a frightened, vengeful fool to stop. The most dangerous kind.

Jericho arrived at his office less than an hour later. His hair was still wet from a second shower and his sooty uniform had been replaced by one as fastidious as usual. Yancey Hamilton was waiting for him, lounging in a chair by his desk.

"Good mornin', Sheriff Jericho." Yancey's greeting was an exaggerated Southern drawl.

"Morning, Yancey." Jericho flipped his hat onto a peg and stepped behind his desk. "I assume that not-so-happy look on your face means the news you have on Maria Elena's car isn't good."

Yancey tossed a sheaf of papers onto his desk and folded his hands over his lean midriff. An unusual scowl distorted the lines of his rugged face. "If you call no news bad news, you got it."

"No news." Jericho sat heavily in his chair, pulling the papers in question closer. "What, exactly, does that mean?"

"First of all, as we suspected, there was nothing else around. Meaning no other explosives tucked away for a surprise bang. The area was clean," Yancey explained in a concise voice a direct opposite from his drawled greeting. "Second, your guy used a simple device. So simple a kid could build it. Everything he used can be found in any hardware store.

"Or worse, any giant retailer." Green eyes that recalled Maria's beguiling robe stared directly into Jericho's. "We can both bet our last dollar, anyone smart enough to keep it this simple wasn't fool enough to use a credit card, or write a check."

"Then you have nothing?" Though this was exactly what he expected, Jericho's mood plummeted. He'd hoped a fool would make a fool's mistakes.

"There is one chance."

Jericho was instantly alert. One chance was better than none. "Tell me."

"One of my men found a glove. Not latex like physicians or dentists or other medical folk wear, a thin plastic thing. The cheap, flimsy, light usage sort." Yancey offered the straw cautiously.

"You're looking for signs of chemicals, maybe a fingerprint from the inside," Jericho ventured. "Which means you'll be taking it back to your lab."

As Yancey shook his head, silver-streaked black hair he'd gathered with a leather cord at his nape gleamed under fluorescent lights. Silver and black, again reminding Jericho of Maria. "I'd rather send it to Simon's people. Our lab is good, even top-notch, but I don't have to tell you, his is the best."

Jericho didn't need an explanation, or a last name. He'd worked a time or two with Simon McKinzie and his fabled Black Watch. Now, it would seem, so had Yancey. Jericho didn't ask how Yancey knew of his association with The Watch. Men and women recruited by Simon asked questions but rarely answered them.

"It might take a little longer," Yancey continued. "But you may get answers you wouldn't anywhere else."

Jericho played a hunch. "The glove is already on its way to Simon, isn't it?"

Yancey grinned, his teeth a flash of white in his craggy face. "By courier, last night." Sobering, he added, "It's still a long shot, Jericho. This guy's a smart cookie. The scene is clueless. There was nothing, nada, zip.

"My crew thinks he could walk in wet sand and leave no footprints. He's either smart or a lucky devil. One can be as bad for an investigation as the other."

Gripping his hands as they lay on his desk, Jericho scowled. "He may be smart, he may be lucky. But he's also a fool, a desperate fool. So desperate that he just might have tipped his hand when he didn't need to."

"Desperate and a fool. Not a good combination." Yancey sighed. "Want to tell me what this is all about?"

"No." Softening his tone, Jericho explained, "It's something that goes back a long way, involving a case before my time as sheriff."

"Before your time, maybe. But something to do with your lady." Shrewd green eyes watched Jericho intently. "It was her rental and the only car in the lot, so this wasn't a mistake. And Miss Delacroix is your lady, isn't she, Jericho?"

"Is it that obvious?"

"Very."

Jericho laughed, but there was no amusement in his eyes. "You never were one to mince words, Hamilton."

"Waste of time and breath."

"Then I won't waste mine in explanations, except to say, Maria Elena *was* my lady. Once."

"Once, huh?" Yancey uncoiled from his chair like a steel spring. He was lean, yet muscular, without an ounce of fat. His eyes were calm. No one had ever seen them any other way. Nor his hand anything but steady.

Jericho thought the man uncoiled like a steel spring because he had nerves of steel. Even when he was disabling a bomb.

"Your lady…has a nice ring to it." Yancey mused in his slow drawl. "My guess is she will be again, Sheriff Jericho."

"Maybe." Jericho kept his tone neutral.

Yancey lifted a shoulder and grinned. "Yeah. Maybe, as soon as we get this matter squared away. Might take some time, though. A generic bomber using generic stuff presents a mite of a problem.

"But I think your lady's good for the time." At Jericho's quick, startled look, he laughed. "I'm not psychic, buddy. I watch the news, I've seen Miss Delacroix in action. Who knows better than I the kind of nerve it takes to stand in the middle of exploding bombs with only a microphone and a camera?

"Until Court confirmed she was in his sister's class at the academy, I'd forgotten exactly how old she was. But, even as an academy student, with a name like Delacroix I know she was never a belle of Belle Terre. Even so, this snobbish little city should be damned proud of her. Brave lady, that one. Easy on the eyes, too.

"Give her my regards and my promise that we'll get this guy." Before Jericho could comment, Yancey tossed him another lazy smile and muttered, "See you around."

As quickly as that, Yancey Hamilton was gone.

Spinning his chair in a half circle, Jericho stared at the city sprawling beyond his window. Somewhere out there was the man who had been one of boys who had taken his baby and the life he should have had with Maria Elena.

"But," he vowed, "not again."

Five

In a muted glide the elevator door slid open, and Jericho stepped into the spacious foyer of the third-floor apartment. In the two weeks that had passed since Maria's car burned, he'd become a frequent and familiar visitor to the inn.

The focus of the protection surrounding Maria had shifted. Changed rather than lessened in degree. With some sophisticated additions to the elevator under Adams Cade's direction, what had once been a simple convenience now required a password and a key for access. Cullen no longer stationed himself by the gliding door, and Maria could enjoy a modicum of privacy.

In rotation, Court, or one of his regular replacements from the force, still stood watch. One by the first-floor elevator landing. More were scattered near the entrances of the ground floor. But most of Jericho's small staff was assigned to stand watch over the gardens and the stretch of the river that bordered the sprawling, secluded property.

Though he went about his duties as head steward of everything happening at the Inn at River Walk, Cullen was never far away.

As he considered this unique man, Jericho smiled, an expression that had become rarer than rare in these weeks. The burly islander, descendant of the fierce warriors of the South Pacific, had taken Maria into his keeping with all the tenderness and concern he lavished on Eden. Watching him with the two women was like a watching a mother hen with two chicks under her wing instead of one.

When Maria first insisted on staying in Belle Terre, Jericho had opposed her decision, both as sheriff and lover. He'd been as uneasy, at first, when she chose to stay on at the inn, rather than with him. Now, he realized the inn was her best and safest choice.

His home was secluded, if not isolated. Tucked into a grove of palms and palmettos, it sat apart on a small promontory created by the convoluted twists and turns of one of the many estuaries wandering along the mainland coast. His closest neighbors were barely within shouting distance. Though the coastline of the jutting point was private, beachcombers were not prohibited. They came, at times, to the pristine shore, yet were rare. Unless his unsuspecting mother or *Grandmère* dropped off a cake or his favorite sugar cookies, Maria would have been alone, and too far from aid.

In the beginning, he'd been too disturbed by her decision to recognize the wisdom of her choice. Not anymore. Though in his official capacity as sheriff, he would breathe easier if she were hundreds of miles away, Jericho admitted he looked forward to coming home to Maria each day…wherever she was.

Puzzled, now, by a hollow silence, he paused at the door leading from the foyer. Downstairs, Eden had greeted him at the door and taken his hat, assuring him he was expected in Maria's secure and comfortable third-floor lodging. Usually, at this hour of evening, the spacious room would be ablaze with lights from many small lamps, and there would be soothing music playing. In the midst of it, when Maria heard the muted report of the elevator, she would rush to meet him, eager for his company, anxious to learn what the investigation had discovered.

Today, beyond the small circle of light spilling from a single lamp, gloom filled the doorways and gathered in corners in the end of twilight. In a room usually filled with life, there was no movement, no sound. The place was as still and quiet as a tomb.

The silence sent a shard of apprehension rushing through Jericho. Instinctively, his hand moved to the revolver strapped at his hip. With his fingers hovering over it, he stepped cautiously into the stillness. Other than the tranquil gardens, or the banks of the ever changing river, this pleasant room, with skylights added in Eden's renovations, was Maria's favorite place.

As a rule the room was pleasantly, but not rigidly, in order. Today there were books and papers stacked on every available surface. But if a strange chaos reigned, his trained survey determined it was orderly chaos. And likely Maria's, not the destructive upheaval of violent intrusion.

Relaxing enough to take his hand from his weapon, Jericho glanced down at the table before the sofa, where a sketch pad and pen lay as if they'd just been put down for a moment. Before he could absorb the meaning of the lines and shadings on the open page, the familiar glide of a closet door drew him to Maria's bedroom.

"Jericho," she cried as his towering bulk filled the door. "I didn't hear you come in." With an array of clothing folded in her arms, she crossed the room to him, rising on tiptoe for his kiss. "Are you early?"

"Actually, I'm late," he answered as he looked from Maria to the bed and the open suitcases resting on it. "It's after seven, Maria Elena."

"Oh my. I lost track of time." With a huff, she blew a stray lock from her eyes and looked down at her jeans and shirt in dismay. "We were going to have dinner in the main dining room downstairs, and I hardly look the part. I can take a quick shower and..." Noticing the stark look on his face, she faltered. "Unless you're too starved to wait."

Jericho's glance moved from Maria to the open cases and back again. "At the moment, I don't have an appetite." His voice was hoarse, his tone strained. "Why don't we have our meal brought up, and then you can tell me what this is all about."

"It does look like mass confusion, I know. But that comes from interrupting one exciting thing with another."

"Judging from what I see—" Jericho tilted his head toward her obvious packing "—I assume you're leaving."

Clutching her clothing, Maria stared up at him. "I am."

"Tonight?" he asked too quietly.

"No, of course not," she denied quickly, and as quietly.

"Tomorrow, then?"

This time she offered no denials. "I was going to tell you after dinner."

He'd wanted her to leave, he knew it would still be for the best. The safest. But after two weeks... With a tense clench of his jaw, Jericho abandoned the thought. He wasn't ready to deal with the prospect of life without Maria.

Deep in his heart, or perhaps in his dreams, he'd begun to believe she felt the same. But, now, from the flush on her cheeks and the dancing sparkle in her eyes, whatever brought about her change of heart was certainly exciting. More exciting than what he offered.

A painful admission, but he wouldn't let his sudden gloom tarnish her delight. "Why don't I go down, find Cullen, tell him of our changed scenerio. When I get back you can tell me your plans."

"Jericho." Maria caught his arm as he turned away. His face was wooden, but she saw beyond the mask. "I thought you would be relieved that I'm going. I thought it was what you wanted."

"It was, and I am, Maria Elena." His expression didn't change with the curt admission. Only his eyes seethed with repressed emotion. "But being glad you're going to safety doesn't mean I won't miss you. Or that I'll forget you, and the times we've shared."

Suddenly Maria smiled, and danced again onto her toes to kiss his cheek. When he understood the reason behind her excitement over this trip, he wouldn't look so sober. "Go speak with Cullen, and when you get back, I have a surprise for you."

As his eyes narrowed, she fluttered her fingers. "Go. While you're with Cullen and making the grounds checks I'm sure you will, I'll finish my packing. Then this last evening can be ours." Another kiss grazed his cheek, another his throat. Her voice was husky in sultry promise. "Only ours, with no interruptions."

This last evening.

Maria's words drummed in Jericho's head as he made his nightly rounds of the property surrounding the Inn at River Walk. A chore complicated by what could be easy access at any point from the river. As proven twice before. The last intrusion resulting in a barely avoided tragedy that nearly cost Adams Cade his life. A situation Jericho was determined wouldn't be repeated. Which, in turn, dictated that most of the surveillance be drawn tightly around the immediate grounds and the house. Two doberman pinschers, trained to perfection, patrolled the river with their handlers nightly.

Normally the presence of the fierce dobies gave Jericho a sense of security. But tonight, beyond quietly calling out his identity, letting his familiar voice alert the animals and his men of his presence on the grounds, he hardly gave either a thought.

Maria was leaving Belle Terre. Now she would be safe.

In verse and chorus, he struggled to keep the thought foremost in his mind. Instead he remembered her flush of excitement. And he couldn't forget that her unwavering determination to stay until the creature who threatened her was apprehended had been swept away in the tide of a new enthusiasm.

As he walked the river's edge, his expression grave, his thoughts brooding, Jericho wondered if he and the joy of their time together had been swept away in that tide, as well.

Eighteen years was a long time for an old flame to smolder. A long time for a teenage attraction to survive. Perchance it hadn't. Perhaps in white-hot passion the flame had burned out.

"For Maria Elena," he muttered, the sound no more than the sigh of a sorrowful breath. "Never for me."

"Evening, boss."

A familiar figure stood beyond a trace of light falling from a distant window. Court Hamilton, of course. A dedicated and capable young man, maturing into his most dependable officer.

"Evening, Court. You're working overtime."

"Yes, sir." Court moved from the shadows to stand beside Jericho. One of the doberman pinschers stood alert and at attention by his side. "Kirk Field's wife is finally having her baby. A girl. She's a stubborn little thing. The baby, I mean. Taking her own sweet time coming into this world."

"A little girl?" Jericho's mind reached back eighteen years to another summer night, and another little girl who was never given the chance to take her own sweet time. A baby conceived in love, born too soon to live.

His little girl, whose mother was leaving him tomorrow. Perhaps because the love had died, too.

Jericho couldn't dwell on the past. He couldn't brood on the future. Not with so much at stake in the present. "So," he said softly. "With the baby taking her time, you stepped in for Kirk."

"Yes, sir." Jericho heard the amiable dismissal in Court's tone. "I didn't think you'd mind, and it seemed the decent thing to do. Every man ought to be with his wife when his baby's born."

"If he can. If his wife and baby's condition allow it." Conditions hadn't allowed anything but desperation and despair with Maria and his child.

Court laughed, untroubled. "I think the only condition that exists here is that the little lady isn't too eager to join a gaggle of four boys. Looks like Kirk's basketball team is going to have a female for point guard."

"You think she'll run the show, do you?"

Court laughed again. "Do you doubt it, sir? The youngest and the only girl? Sure. They'll all spoil her rotten and let her rule the house and their lives."

"Probably." Jericho steered the subject from babies and little girls. "You do this a lot, don't you, Court? Take extra duty for your fellow officers, that is."

"Some. I'm single, with no emotional attachments and no demands on my spare time. If I can help, I do." Court's gaze lifted to the third-floor balcony, and the light streaming dully through the unshuttered, open door. "But tonight is as much for her as for Kirk. I don't want to see her hurt anymore."

*Her…*Maria.

"Anymore." Jericho repeated, wondering what prompted the younger officer's comment. No one in Belle Terre knew the truth or the tragedy of the night Maria was attacked. No one except the boys, old Doc Wilson and the small staff of his tiny private hospital. Of those few, only he and Maria and the doctor knew about the baby. With a soft spot in his heart for Maria, the kindly physician had seen to that. Doc Wilson died several years after Maria left Belle Terre. But not before he gave Maria's medical records to Jericho.

Even in extremis, the gracious and compassionate old man was concerned for the reputation and well-being of Maria, the undeserving heir of the Delacroix legacy of shame and hate.

"Yes, sir—anymore." Court Hamilton's answer drew Jericho back from the brink of intolerable anguish. "Don't know what happened to her, or when, but it left a powerful hurt in her eyes. I wouldn't want to see this bastard add to it."

Jericho stifled a start of unwarranted surprise. He knew Court Hamilton was twenty-seven, maybe twenty-eight. But his youthful, untried look always beguiled even his closest elders into foolishly underestimating him. "He won't, Court. Not so long as I have men of your caliber in my command."

"Thank you, sir. But it's just part of my job."

"Maybe." Jericho agreed, but he was more than grateful men like Court carried their responsibilities to a higher level.

The doberman had stood like an image carved of onyx. Tall, sleek, his clipped ears erect, his black coat gleaming in a stray beam of the moon. Now his muscular body shivered as an errant tide set the *River Runner* rocking. Sending the bow of the inn's trim craft bumping against its dock as it wallowed in the lapping swale.

With eyes as dark as coal searching the shore, the dog was eager to be about his duties. As Jericho knew the magnificent animal should be. And his handler. With a touch on Court's shoulder he conveyed gratitude both knew the sheriff wouldn't speak.

His personal inspection complete, loathe to keep the rarely but well matched partners from their rounds, Jericho took his leave of them. He'd almost reached the inn when the deep, young baritone floated out of the shadows again.

"Sir?" Court waited until Jericho paused and turned. "Would you give Miss Delacroix my best? Tell her no crazy stalker will get to her if I can help it."

"I'll do that, Court." He couldn't see man or dog, but he knew they hadn't gone far. He knew they wouldn't until the doberman was satisfied that no human intruder disturbed the *Runner*. "Maria Elena will be glad to know you're here, watching over her."

For the first time since he stepped off the elevator on the third floor, Jericho Rivers smiled in the late summer darkness.

"Officer Hamilton's a nice young man." Maria stood at the open doorway, looking down into the garden where twilight had completely given way to night. Trees and plants were only great black shapes in the failing light. But Southern moonlit nights could be as entrancing in their own way as the dawn and morning. "From his speech and his gentlemanly manner, he sounds as if he might have been one of Lady Mary's star pupils."

"Probably. His sister was." When he came in from the personal patrol Maria predicted, Jericho had put aside his weapon and spoke of Court, conveying the young deputy's assurance.

In a perverse way, Jericho was deliberately delaying the inevitable discussion of her departure. "Almost every kid in Belle Terre was exposed to Lady Mary's teachings. Many still are."

"Even some from the wrong families, like me," Maria added softly. "You haven't forgotten, have you?"

Without waiting for an answer, lifting her face to the evening stars, she murmured, "Lady Mary was the first person who treated me as if I mattered. She made me believe I could be a person of value. In private classes, after all the rest of you had gone, she insisted I must be. If for no other reason, to prove a Delacroix could make a worthwhile contribution somewhere, somehow."

Facing Jericho, her expression reflecting wonder at Lady Mary's kindness even now, Maria asked, "Who would believe the impoverished descendant of one of the low country's wealthiest planters would take an interest and believe so strongly in the daughter of a Delacroix?

"But Mary Alston did. When every penny counted toward keeping her a step away from abject poverty, she taught me as if I were one of you. Expecting only a sense of self-respect and a desire to be someone as payment." Maria's arms were crossed, her hands trailed from her elbows to her shoulders and back. A soft smile touched her lips. "That was the beginning. The first time I had reason to believe in myself."

"Then there was another, Maria." Jericho had no clue who

her next benefactor was, yet he knew there had to have been one. "And next came the academy."

"Another?" Maria shook her head. "Not one. Two. Two strangers who, with anonymous generosity, invested in Lady Mary Alston's trust, and in my life. Once, because he was kind to me, I asked Doc Wilson if he was the one."

"Was he?" It made sense to Jericho that he would be.

"He said my benefactors were friends of Mary Alston. But he wouldn't give their names. Through the years only three kind ladies and Doc knew how the daughter of the town drunk could afford to study at the exclusive Belle Terre Academy. No one else ever understood why I was there." Her melodious voice grew thoughtful, if a little strained. "Sometimes not even little Maria."

"Why, love? Why did you doubt?"

Maria didn't answer for a moment. From a tree beyond the balcony a mockingbird sang his heart out to the night, the sound of it filled the room. Then all was still again.

"No one thought I belonged, Jericho." Maria's gaze held his. A tender smile lifted the corners of her mouth. "Except you."

"You were the smartest in our class, Maria Elena. Of course you belonged." He could have gone on with the list, but enumerating superlatives would only bring back memories of the resentment and jealousy she'd encountered because of her looks and her abilities.

As she read his expression, her smile became a look of sorrow. "Which only served to alienate my classmates even more. Some merely resented it. Some hated me for it."

Spinning back to the open door, she looked beyond the balcony. As if it sensed the downward spiral of her mood, the mockingbird didn't serenade the woman or the night again.

"He's out there, Jericho." Maria folded her arms more tightly about her. "The one who hated me most is out there now, wondering when I might remember his face."

With her fingers clutching the soft flesh of her arms in a

cruel grip, she whispered into the rise of a gentle river breeze. "Where are you? Who are you? Why can't I remember?"

"Don't, Maria." Jericho moved toward her, but stopped short when she visibly tensed. Bereft in his need to touch her, to hold and comfort her, he implored softly, "Don't torture yourself with this. Tomorrow you'll be gone. Then all this will be behind you."

When she faced him, the flush had long given way to pallor, the sparkle in her eyes to dark intensity. "It won't ever be behind me, Jericho, no more than you've put it behind you. Why else do you still put flowers on an unmarked grave on a midsummer day?"

"Because I'm here, Maria." Jericho said nothing more. There was no need in denying the obvious.

With a long regretful sigh, Maria spoke a dawning understanding. "I never thought…" With a slight bow of her head, her voice faded, then grew stronger. "Until now, I never realized that maybe that's where I've been fortunate. Though it never stops hurting, perhaps it wasn't as bad somewhere else. Except for law school and your time in the pros, you've had to live here, Jericho. Here, in Belle Terre, where the memories live."

"My time in pro football was only a means to an end, financing a degree I've never really used after all. But I didn't have to return to Belle Terre after I passed the boards and quit football. Then it was my choice."

"Your choice," she repeated. As opposed to her choice to leave this place of heartache? But she didn't dispute him. Instead, she wondered aloud, "You can call a destroyed knee a choice?"

"My knee only precipitated the inevitable. This is home, Maria." A home he would have left without a backward look when she was seventeen and he, eighteen. If she'd asked him to go with her.

"Your home, Jericho. And mine, now." Leaving the open door, Maria crossed to the table still piled high with books and sketches. "This assignment, reporting a little skirmish in the Middle East, will be my last. It isn't one I would have been scheduled to take, except I know some of the people involved.

"Even so, at first I refused. But the network is so eager to have someone with a semblance of knowledge of the thought processes of Josef, the rebel leader, that they've agreed to terminate my contract with the completion of this one last jaunt."

"Jaunt? The Middle East?" Jericho nearly strangled on the words. "You consider walking into a nest of vipers—familiar vipers or not—with only a microphone and a camera, a jaunt?"

"I've done it before." A lift of her shoulders dismissed the danger. "How else do you think I became acquainted with the man known only as Josef—which, of course, is not his real name.

"Where do you think I saw so many cars blown to cinders that I learned to recognize the method? Even the intent?

"This is what I do, Jericho. What I've done more times than you can know. Because I have, and because the network and certain organizations in Washington see this small acquaintance as their only hope of resolving this conflict before too many lives are lost, I've been asked to go.

"One last time, Jericho," she promised softly. "One."

Simon. The name leaped unbidden into Jericho's mind. Could it be Maria Elena was working for the legendary leader of The Black Watch? With piercing eyes he studied the slender woman who stood before him, seeing her for the first time as more than the frightened girl of his memories. More than his lover. Perhaps more than the competent professional she'd become.

Yes, he decided as shackles fell from his vision. The association would be plausible. Maybe even likely. For the wily Simon McKinzie was never one to miss an opportunity. But if it should be true, the venerable leader of The Black Watch had found the low country to be a veritable cornucopia of unmissed opportunities.

As sheriff, Jericho had worked with the super secret organization, and he was often informed of an agent's presence in the area based on "need to know" criteria. Yancey Hamilton's association with the Scot had been left unclear, yet came as no real surprise. There were others of The Watch who had come and gone. Others who would come and go in the future. But now Maria?

Whatever his suspicions and fears, he couldn't ask her not to accept the assignment. She'd taken that right from him long ago. A right that being temporary lovers couldn't give back.

"What time do you leave?" he asked with a sense of déjà vu, as if this were his apartment and her car still waited at the museum.

"My flight to Washington is scheduled for four. There will be day or so of briefings. Once they're completed, if all else falls into place, I should leave the country immediately."

She spoke as if preparing for entry into a dangerous rebel skirmish was a common occurrence for her. Suddenly, Jericho knew that it was. He was seeing a side of Maria that he hadn't seen before. A side neither he nor the rest of the viewers of her national newscasts suspected existed.

"How long will you be gone?" He tried not to think of the risk, no matter that she was a professional and clearly a seasoned one.

"Six weeks. Less, if we're lucky. Longer, if we're not."

"We?"

"I won't go alone, Jericho. Not until I meet with Josef. *If* I meet with Josef," she amended calmly. "Then, by the agreement, my contract will be fulfilled, and I can return to Belle Terre."

"Then you're truly coming back?" For once, Jericho, a man who knew himself and his duties beyond question, didn't know what he should think, how he should feel.

"Of course I'm coming back." Linking an arm through his, she led him to a seat on the sofa. "Look."

Jericho glanced at the sheaf of drawings she thrust at him, but at a glance, he could make no real sense of them. "House plans?"

"Not just any house, Jericho. The plans of Lady's Hall."

"Lady's Hall?" He'd heard the name, but not in a long time, and at the moment he drew a blank.

"It's no wonder you don't remember. The house has rarely been called by its real name." Maria spread the plans on the table, making the size and style of the house more apparent.

"The Delacroix house?"

"Exactly." She rewarded his belated recognition with a beaming smile. "The Delacroix house on Fancy Row. My house."

"Yours?" Jericho had leaned over to study the drawings at closer range. Now he sat back to stare in surprise at Maria. "The Delacroix house belongs to you? I know it has been for sale for a long while, but no one... You bought it."

"I was going to surprise you with it when the plans for the renovations were complete." With a lift of her shoulders, she dismissed her scheme. "The trouble with Josef changed that."

"Renovations." The plans made perfect sense now. "You've bought the Delacroix house, and now you plan to refurbish it."

"Actually, Eden will do it. Or at least oversee those who do. With Adams's help, of course."

"Adams knows about this? And he approves?"

"Of course." Maria was surprised he would even ask. "I wouldn't think of involving Eden in the project if Adams wasn't in favor of it, as well. Luckily, he thinks it will be good for Eden."

"Tell me how, when she's expecting a baby."

Maria realized he was far from pleased with her plan. Patiently, because his opinion was the most important, she explained. "Interior design is Eden's field of expertise, and what she loves. Added to that, she loves the architecture of the houses on Fancy Row. It's her dream to see all of them restored to their former glory. Having a hand in it will please her mightily. As Adams sees it, the happier Eden is, the easier this pregnancy will go.

"We've been planning this the whole two weeks. She knows what I want, and how to do it. I've given her power of attorney, and when all the legalities are settled, she will begin. But, first of all, she has promised she won't overtire herself.

"I believe her. Eden wants Adams's baby too badly to jeopardize it. You should know that, Jericho."

"I do. It's just that…"

"You don't want me to do this." Maria finished for him.

"It's better to say I don't understand why you're doing it."

"I'm a Delacroix." Her chin tilted at a proud angle. "I've finally learned it's nothing to be ashamed of. Because I am what I am, and who I am, I want to live in the house of the Delacroix. Can you not understand that, Jericho? Can you not be happy for me?"

"How? Considering the circumstances?" With more questions than answers, Jericho worried that having a Delacroix back on Fancy Row would stir up trouble, even though most of a century had passed since any of the beautiful courtesans had occupied the house.

Lady's Hall had been the finest house on the row. Now it was the shabbiest derelict. Though structurally sound, the brick walls had been defaced, windows broken, then boarded up. Doors were splintered and left to hang at cocked angles. God only knew what lived there at times. Animals, tramps, runaways, druggies.

And resentment. The resentment of some of Belle Terre's finest still lived on Fancy Row. In a Southern town steeped in tradition and in worship of the past, it thrived.

"Jericho?" She waited until he looked away from the plans

and met her gaze. ''Are we quarreling? Is this how it's going to be between us when I leave?''

''No.'' He shook his head. Then, with a sense of desperation, he drew her into his arms. ''It will be like this.''

Later, when Cullen rapped at the door, there was no answer. Smiling to himself, the islander set the tray bearing a cold supper on a table in the foyer and left as quietly as he'd come.

Six

Sheriff Jericho Rivers was angry. No. He knew that what his men were witnessing went beyond anger. What they saw and what they were hearing was deep, cold rage. Rage that would have been cause for concern for any one of them, if it were turned in their direction.

This was a blazing revelation of fury that had seethed and smoldered for two weeks. Untamed emotion he couldn't allow to supersede his first priority—protecting Maria. But now she was gone. Before the dew dried on the grass, far before he was ready, she had left him.

By now, her plane would be touching down in Washington. Soon the woman he loved and would protect with his life would prepare for top secret meetings in the nation's capital. Then for a siege in a remote country torn by rebellion and bigotry.

With her hushed goodbye whispering through his mind and the touch of her kiss lingering on his lips, in the throes of regret and a tone harsh with impotent fury, Jericho imparted the little he knew of the bombing to his men. Laying aside the notes he'd ignored, he searched the faces of those summoned to this briefing. The men gathered there were his own men, with a few from other agencies, selected and requested for their expertise in specialized areas. Dedicated professionals to a man.

Qualities that instilled pride and confidence. And comfort. Except, this time, there would be no comfort for Jericho until the threat to Maria was ended.

His grim expression grew desolate. In him lay a violent storm ready to wreak its wrath. This was a mood few had ever witnessed. A man none had ever seen. "Find him," he concluded at last, his voice harsh in the hollow quiet that had fallen like a pall over the room. "I don't care what it takes, find him."

His gray eyes, almost black with cold, unrelenting purpose, touched on each man who sat watching him. Gripping the lectern to still the tremor that seized him each time he thought of the burned-out hull of Maria's car, he continued, "We were lucky this time. Toby Parker sustained only minor burns, some bruises, and a broken arm. Next time might be different. The next person caught in the crossfire could be seriously injured or killed."

"Sir." Court Hamilton braved Jericho's uncommon wrath.

"Deputy Hamilton?" Jericho recognized him tersely.

"You say next time. Since this so-called stalker is targeting Miss Delacroix, does that mean she's coming back?"

"Yes, it means she's coming back."

"But, sir, the stalker only threatened her here. Clearly, she's safer somewhere else, so why come back?"

"Because this is her home, Hamilton," Jericho snapped in a dangerous tone. *Because she's my wife, my love, my life.*

If all eyes were on Jericho before, now they were riveted on him, seeking answers for his strange attitude, for the mood of his response. Answers that, plainly, weren't imminent. In the crowded room concerned silence plummeted to a deeper level. The stillness grew eerie as the perplexed men waited.

Jericho didn't notice. Maria and keeping her safe were all he had room for in his world. All he could think of. "You've been divided into teams, given assignments. Follow through. Check and double check. Then check again. We have no clues, no lead, but they're out there. Find them." With a look that set hairs prickling at the backs of innocent necks, he repeated, "Find him."

Abruptly, he dismissed his men. One by one, with none of their usual banter, they filed from the briefing room. Then he was alone, but he didn't stir or look away from his hands as he continued to grip the lectern in a bone-punishing force.

"Maria Elena."

He'd lost her once. One small error, one coincidental moment, a change of plans, and he could have lost her a second time. If the bomber wasn't found, next time might be forever.

Jericho straightened from the worn stand, rising to his great height, his gaze straying to the window and to the main street of Belle Terre as it sprawled toward the bay. This was his town, his to protect. It was his duty, as well, to keep safe all who lived and visited within his jurisdiction. And he would.

To an unknown man, he vowed, "You won't hurt her again."

The rage that had lived inside him for two weeks like a caged tiger was wild and free at last. Jericho couldn't curb it. For the first time in his life, he wouldn't try.

Moving away from the lectern, his hands fisted at his sides, he stared for a moment longer at the streets of Belle Terre. Was *he* out there? Was he waiting in fear of Maria Elena's return? Jericho's stare swept over the street once more, lingering on doorways and corners. As his look turned colder, harder, more dangerous, a harsh breath shuddered through him. Then, wheeling sharply about, he left the room without a backward glance.

In forbidding, unapproachable silence, he stalked through

the main office with its occupied desks arranged in neat rows. As he passed them by, secretaries, clerks, and officers looked up in surprise. One by one their attention turned from their tasks, and friendly banter halted as they watched a stranger pass.

The door to his private office closed with a solid thud, shutting Jericho away from their startled stares. A shocked silence continued a few seconds longer. Then the whispers began.

"Well, well, well, it happened, at last," Yancey Hamilton drawled as he spun his chair away from a window to watch Jericho curiously. "Even the mighty have a breaking point."

Jericho stopped short, his back nearly touching the closed door. The frown on his face darkened. "What does that remark mean?"

"It means I've been waiting for years to see the monumental control of Jericho Rivers slip its traces." With a tilt of his head, Yancey indicated the direction of the briefing room. "Now I have."

Jericho crossed to his desk and sank into his own chair, his look meeting Yancey's. "Have you?"

"Yep." Propping a heel on a stool, and clasping his hands over his middle, the smaller of the two men smiled. "I don't think I would want to be this guy when we catch him."

Before Jericho could comment, Yancey swung his feet to the floor and straightened in his chair. Hands resting on his knees, his green gaze probing Jericho's, he said, quietly, "Want to tell me what this is all about?"

A raised hand turned palm outward forestalled Jericho's reply. "And don't give me the stalker crap. We both know there's more to this than some nutcase with a crush on a TV personality."

Jericho's gaze narrowed. "What makes you so sure?"

"I'm sure because I talked to the lady herself." Yancey didn't look away from Jericho. His astute gaze swept over grim features and the bleak look in stony gray eyes. "And, because from what she tells me, this guy doesn't fit the pattern.''

"What pattern is that?" Jericho settled back in his chair, but looked no more relaxed than he had before.

Rolling his eyes at having each of his questions consistently answered with another question, Yancey replied, "By the time a stalker reaches the point where he acts out his frustrations—usually the frustrations of being rejected—there first has to have been contact. Overtures, rebuffed or ignored. Overtures that can be anything. Letters, phone calls, gifts, flowers, you name it.''

"So?" Jericho's chair tilted forward as he concentrated on Yancey. "What's your point?"

"Maria said there'd been nothing of the sort. No sign of a stalker. Nothing to refuse that would tip him over the edge. Not one phone call, one letter," Yancey enumerated. "Not even one posie.''

When Jericho remained silent, Yancey said nothing, tension stretching taut between the two men. Only the creak of leather and Jericho's resigned sigh ended the stalemate. "You're right, Yance. This isn't an ordinary stalker.''

"What else is new!" Yancey snorted. "What's ordinary about any stalker, except his pattern?"

"There is no pattern here." Curling his fingers into hard fists, Jericho added, "Except that Maria Elena is the target.''

"Bingo!" Yancey rose from his chair with the same coiled-spring action as always. With nerves of steel, he was steadier than the proverbial rock, yet quicker than lightning. As Jericho watched him, he didn't doubt the man could outstare, outwait, or outstrike a rattler, if the need arose.

"That means it's happened before," Yancey said thoughtfully, his intuitive mind searching for possibilities and probabilities. "Yes," he said again as it fell neatly into place. "That's the answer. It has to be.''

With hair like Maria's gleaming in reminder, he crossed to Jericho's desk. Leaning on it, he muttered bitterly, "He's come after her before. But not recently enough for her to connect it with the bombing of her car. At least, not at first. Not when we talked.''

Yancey glared down at the man who was his friend. ''Well?''

Jericho met the challenge steadily, his expression revealing nothing. ''This is your show, Yance. You tell me.''

''Dammit, man!'' Yancey's Southern drawl disappeared. The clipped voice of the professional spoke now. ''You called *me*. You asked for my help in this. And I can tell you, buddy, you're angrier than I've ever seen you. Angrier than you would let yourself be if you could stop it. But you can't, can you? That tells me you aren't thinking like the Jericho Rivers I know.''

He leaned on the desk again, in rare confounded concern. ''The site's clean, Jericho. A smart ten-year-old kid could have made the device that set the car off. He could have made it with things lying around the house, or picked up at the neighborhood hardware store. Because of its simplicity, the components are nearly beyond tracking. Unless I know something about the perpetrator. If I know enough, I can crawl into his mind, think like he does, maybe even go where he's gone.''

Standing erect again, Yancey's stare dueled with that of his mute friend. ''Then maybe we'll find someone who remembers something. Then, maybe another someone who remembers something else. It could be only bits and pieces, but in putting them together, they just might fit. Then we'll have a clue to trace.''

''Maybe?''

''Yeah, I said maybe. It's a long shot even if I know all the facts. But hopefully better than the blank I've drawn with what I know now.'' Drawing a breath, Yancey lifted a shoulder in a weary shrug. ''I need more information. I think you have it. Think on it. Consider the alternatives if you keep me in the dark.

''I'll give you a day, Jericho. If I haven't heard from you

by then, I'm outta here. There are other places and other ways I can put my time to better use.''

Yancey stalked to the door. He was angry and frustrated. But through it all, he'd been his usual steady self. And as calm, deep down, beneath the unusual display of anger.

"I don't need a day, Yance."

Yancey paused with his hand on the latch. He waited.

Jericho's look was grave. "I don't need a day to decide."

"Do I go, or do I stay, Jericho?"

"You stay."

Wordlessly, Yancey returned to his chair. His keen gaze was fixed on Jericho, before Jericho spoke again. "You were right. This has happened before. It happened here in Belle Terre. When she was seventeen, Maria Elena was attacked by a gang of boys. There were three or four, she could never remember which. Nor can I."

"She couldn't recognize any of them?" Yancey asked.

"They wore ski masks."

"Why? What reason would they have for attacking her? Robbery? Rape?" Catching the look that flickered in Jericho's face, Yancey grimaced. "Good Lord! Surely not to rape her?"

"The threat was made."

Yancey shuddered and closed his eyes. With a shake of his head, he looked back at Jericho. "Because she was a Delacroix."

"How did you guess?"

Hearing the note of surprise in Jericho's voice, Yancey laughed. It was a bitter laugh. "Don't sound so shocked, my friend. Have you forgotten I spent the first seventeen years of my ill-begotten life in rebellion against just such hypocrisy?"

"I remember. Before you left, you cut a wide swath through any number of pretensions, Yance. For all the good it did, you might as well have been tilting at windmills."

"The power of the self-righteous prevails, while the rebel self-destructs?" Yancey's grin was humorless and world-weary.

"Something like that," Jericho agreed. It was the same battle he'd fought, in another way. His own way.

"It never changes, does it, Jericho? Despite a rebel like me, and strong, genuinely good people like you, after who knows how long, some of Belle Terre's illustrious, pristine citizens still point the judgmental finger. They hate pretty little girls who can't help what some woman with the same name did generations ago. What's worse, they infect their children with the same hate."

"Hell," Yancey mocked, "if they knew I was back in town, they'd probably still keep their daughters under lock and key."

"Bad Boy Yancey Hamilton," Jericho mused. He was only fifteen and Yancey seventeen when the older boy ran away. But even at fifteen, Jericho understood that Yancey wasn't a bad boy as much as a rebel. Making matters worse, he was smarter than most of his instructors at the Belle Terre Academy, and had little patience with their pretentious opinions. His greatest pleasure in class was exposing their stupidity and ostentatious manners. "You were so busy with your own vendetta, and Maria was so much younger, I'm surprised you remember her."

"We had a lot in common, Jericho. My father was a drunk, her father was a drunk. The forgiving difference was that mine was a well-connected, wealthy, *genteel* drunk."

Yancey lifted a finger in exaggerated pantomime, deliberately reminding Jericho of the pompous instructors the rebel had spent his youth debunking. "That's important, you know. Historic connections, wealth, and gentility excuse a multitude of sins in this town. But sharing the common denominator of drunken parents isn't the real reason I remember Maria."

"Somehow I didn't think so."

Yancey smiled for real then. "I was never a cradle robber, but I had an eye for budding beauties. Maria Delacroix was one of the prettiest. She lived up to her promise."

Jericho's head tilted in agreement. His thoughts wandered again to Maria. Had her plane landed? Would she be safe on this assignment? Safer than he'd kept her in Belle Terre. His lips twisted in renewed anger as Yancey continued his narrative.

"Now that the lady of questionable heritage has come home again, at least one of the masked boys is living in fear that she might recognize him. Or remember and destroy his life." Yancey cast a glance at a silent Jericho. His smile was a parody now, but his voice was still clipped, still precise. The professional at work. "How am I doing so far?"

Jericho's chair creaked again as he drew another long breath. A ray of sun falling through a window cast his face in shadows even as it illuminated Yancey's world-worn but handsome features. "Batting a thousand. If you were a young renegade in school, you were the smartest, most intuitive renegade around. That hasn't changed."

"A matter of opinion," Yancey muttered softly, returning to his summation. "So, our boy, who has become a man, probably with a family and a lot to lose, decided to scare her away. We've all concluded, given the method and the time frame, that he didn't intend to harm her."

"Agreed." Finding little comfort in agreeing, Jericho felt compelled to add, "Not yet."

"Two things aren't clear about this." Yancey could only see Jericho's dark shape framed in stark relief against the sun-glazed window. But he heard a multitude of emotions, he'd seen the rage. Savage rage sane men of Jericho's size avoided at all cost. As Jericho always had, until now. Until Maria Delacroix was involved.

"First of all, where was Maria the night of the incident? Why was her car left in the parking lot?" Yancey narrowed his eyes, trying to glean a semblance of reaction from Jericho's posture. But as the light spilled past the desk and slanted across Yancey's face, his laser-like eyes were blinded, and could read nothing.

"Second," with an exasperated sigh, he continued almost too quietly, "where the hell do you figure in this equation?"

Jericho heard, but he didn't respond. He didn't move. Even so, the same blinding, slanting ray of the sun played across the plain of his broad shoulders, defining their width and strength beneath the immaculate khaki shirt. Like a playful imp, it grazed the surface of his desk, painting his hands with a shimmer of light, setting the gold band agleam with reflections of its fire. And still, his face was obscured.

Jericho's gaze was drawn to the light and the ring Maria had given him on a sunny day like this. His shoulders lifted, his face turned. His strong profile, cast in shades of light and dark, didn't alter even as his decision was made.

"Maria Elena was with me the night her car burned."

In thirty-eight years Yancey Hamilton had seen everything, done everything. He'd been shockproof since his early teens. Jericho's quiet statement threatened his trademark calm as little ever had. A finely drawn brow lifted over eyes that had turned to dark jade in the shifting light. His lips were a restrained line. "Maria was with you? Who knew this?"

"Anyone who cared to notice, or spy, as the case may be." Now that he'd said the words, Jericho felt a weight lift from his heart. "She left the museum gala with me."

"And stayed the night?" Yancey nailed it down, leaving nothing in this turn of event to chance or misunderstanding.

Jericho's chin angled in admission. "Maria Elena stayed the night." His gray gaze lifted to Yancey's, holding it. "In my bed."

Yancey was silent, his agile mind had reviewed possibilities, even probabilities. He knew there was a strong connection between Jericho and Maria, but he never expected this. "You hadn't seen each other in…what? Fifteen years?"

"Eighteen," Jericho supplied. "Eighteen long, lost years."

"All right." Yancey ran his open palms over the glossy black mane drawn cruelly from his perplexed face. "You hadn't seen Maria in eighteen years…and just like that—" The snap of his fingers sounded like a shot in the small room. "Yeah, just like that she goes home with you for the night?

"That doesn't fit with the Maria I recall." Yancey's head turned in a negative gesture. "Not at all."

"Maria Elena is my wife." Jericho's revelation was spoken hoarsely. Before Yancey could react or question, he explained, "We were married a few weeks before she was attacked."

The sun and the light that played games with them had finally inched beyond the window. Beams falling from its meridian cast no shadows, offered no hiding place for raw emotions.

Studying the strong, handsome face, and the pain he could see at last, Yancey whistled a low note. "Makes sense," he said finally. "Now that I think about it, it makes one helluva lot of sense. The two of you were always good together. Pretty, brainy Maria, the gallant giant Jericho always looking out for her."

At Jericho's look of surprise, Yancey smiled. "Yeah, I saw it. I might have been older and the black sheep, but I wasn't blind. Everybody saw it. But I guess none of us ever thought..." With a gesturing hand, he broke off. "Doesn't matter what any of us thought then. What matters is now.

"Even so, I think this is a story I should hear, my friend." Yancey slipped deeper into his chair. With his hands tented beneath his chin, he regarded Jericho steadily. "And I should hear it from beginning to end."

Yancey didn't swear himself to secrecy, but the unspoken vow was in his tone. Accepting it, Jericho began. "I know," he said, pensively. "Perhaps the telling is long overdue."

A rap sounded at the door before Jericho could answer, Officer O'Brian, the guardian of his privacy, and his self-appointed mother hen, intruded.

Balancing a tray on one hand, with the other she swung the door closed, finishing the task with a shift of an ample hip. She hadn't waited for the first invitation, she didn't wait for a second. Bustling past Yancey, she stopped at Jericho's desk and set down the tray.

With an accusing glance at Yancey, in her best mother hen

tone, she launched into a lecture. "It's well past lunch, and if I know you, breakfast didn't figure in your plans, either."

Hands on her hips, her pale silver hair falling around a careworn face, despite the fact that Jericho was her superior and more than twice her size, she spoke like a scolding mother to a recalcitrant child. "I've brought sandwiches and milk and coffee for you and Mr. Hamilton. There's sugar cookies, compliments of your *grandmère,* as well. And you're going to eat every crumb.

"Brains, even keen brains like yours, work better if they're nourished." Turning on her heel, with a nod to Yancey, O'Brian commanded, "See that he does." Her snapping black glare ranged over Yancey's lean frame as he sprawled in the chair. "As far as that goes, you may not be as big as Jer... As big as sheriff Rivers, but you need fuel, too. For that matter, you could use some meat on your bones, Yancey Hamilton."

When the door shut behind her in a quiet slam, Yancey looked at Jericho in awe. "That was O'Brian. Molly O'Brian!"

"I know."

"She was part of the police department back in my heyday. There were times I saw her more often than I did my mother."

"I know."

"She hates men on general principles."

"Yes."

"But not Jericho Rivers."

"No."

Yancey chuckled then. "There's the story of our lives, Jericho. Women lusted after me, or hated me, for what they thought I was. They all loved you for what you truly are. If O'Brian's any indication, they still do. Especially those of a younger persuasion, I'd bet."

Jericho shrugged aside the comment. "There's never been anyone but Maria Elena, Yancey."

"Because she was the only one who ever mattered?"

"After she left, I searched for her. As well as an eighteen-year-old can search in secret. When I couldn't find her and every avenue closed, I was bitter. I tried to hate her."

"But you couldn't."

"I moved the wedding band she gave me to my right hand and gave it a damned good try. I went looking for a replacement, promising myself that if there was ever anyone I wanted, I'd take it off, forget about Maria Elena, and never put it back on."

Jericho's hand convulsed into a loose fist as it lay on his desk. The gold band, the only jewelry he ever wore, gleamed with the patina of wear and age. "There was never anyone."

Jericho had just solved one of the greatest mysteries of Belle Terre. Through the years, even after his days of rebellion ended, Yancey rarely came home. With a mother whose greatest delight was gossip, even rare visits exposed him to the hottest and longest-running topic of avid interest.

Before he was drafted into pro football, Jericho had been a challenge to the young women of Belle Terre. After he retired, still a source of intrigue with his ever-present gold band and dedicated bachelorhood, the gallant but pleasantly aloof new sheriff had become the object of avid feminine interest.

As reported faithfully and in detail, Yancey knew that Jericho might have been a monk, but never a hermit. The dashing sheriff had escorted ladies to concerts, to plays, even to dinner, then left them on their doorsteps without so much as a kiss. Even so, if there was ever a second date, interest and speculation ran high. Hopes soared, only to fall in the dust.

Jericho Rivers, an obviously normal, healthy, virile man of mystery was an unrepentant bachelor.

"Or so everyone thought," Yancey muttered aloud, wondering what the years of waiting and wondering had been like for Jericho. "Rather than a dedicated bachelor, for all these years, you were dedicated to Maria."

It wasn't a question, and Jericho didn't bother to answer.

The gold band he'd placed on his right hand, and never in all the years removed, answered for him.

"Why, Jericho?" Yancey did ask then. "I think that's the part of this story I need to hear."

"Yes," Jericho agreed softly.

The coffee had grown cold, the milk warm, and the untouched sandwiches were soggy beyond redemption when Jericho finished the story of himself and Maria and sat waiting, saying no more.

"A lost baby girl?" Yancey growled. "Damn them to hell."

"That says it all, doesn't it?"

"In spades. I'm not sure if there's anything in your story I can use, but I'm sure as hell going to try." Yancey unfolded from his chair, grabbed a cup of cold coffee and gulped it down. The cup rattled back into its saucer. "Starting now."

With a salute, he muttered, "I'll call you."

Then Jericho was alone in an office that felt like a cage. In a town that seemed empty without Maria. With an afternoon that stretched endlessly before him.

The house was dark and, in Jericho's mind, echoed with a desolate emptiness when he turned the key and shut off the security alarm. Without switching on a light, he wound his way through the house and up the stairs. In his bedroom, he discarded his shirt, his belt, then sat on the bed to draw off his boots.

O'Brian's guess had been on the mark, and despite her good intention he'd skipped more than one meal.

He'd begun his day by driving Maria to the airport, intending to have breakfast with her in the lobby coffee shop while they waited for her boarding call. But neither of them was hungry. Instead, they'd lingered over shared cups of coffee, content just to be together for the little time left to them.

The boarding call had come too soon. Suddenly she was in

his arms, with tears glittering in her eyes as she rose on tiptoe to meet his kiss. They'd had only two weeks together. But as he held her, wanting to keep her forever, he knew they were weeks that changed his life.

Then she was gone, leaving him with memories of their lovemaking, of long slow kisses and gentle caresses. Of hopes, and sweet dreams, and solemn promises.

Now, at the end of a long, difficult day of sadness and goodbyes, his body cried out for food. Taut muscles ached for the penetrating heat of a steamy shower. But his heart and soul longed only for Maria.

Stretching out on the bed, his arms folded beneath his head, he breathed deeply. He hadn't made love to Maria in his bed in days, but for Jericho the scent of her still drifted from the laundered sheets and in the air. In his mind, it always would.

Wrapped in her remembered scent, he listened to the whisper of the sea and the tap of palmetto fronds against the window. Sounds that always delighted her. Sounds that made her changeable eyes shine with all the colors of enchantment.

As mating with him filled their deep, gray depths with the look of the wonder of love.

Maria had come home. Home to Jericho. She would again.

"In a month," he muttered as he drifted into exhausted sleep. "Maria Elena will be home in a month."

Seven

Hammers pounded in the distance. The sound of their impact shattered a relative quiet as Jericho stepped through the front door and into the foyer of Lady's Hall.

"Yo! Jericho," a painter called from a scaffold far above floor level. "How goes it?"

"Good," he answered back, lying through his teeth as he continued his search for Eden. "Working late, aren't you?"

"The nature of the job when you work for Miss Eden." The painter chuckled in good humor. "If you're lookin' for the boss lady, she's down by the dock with a crew of carpenters. Just follow the sound and you're sure to find her."

"Thanks," Jericho replied. Despite his brooding mood, he was amused by the name. *Boss lady.* A fitting christening, for Eden was the boss and a lady. In spades, as Yancey Hamilton had declared on his last visit to Belle Terre and to Lady's Hall.

Lady's Hall. At least that was one thing that was going as it should, and often even better. In spite of his concerns regarding the wisdom of this project, and his initial lack of enthusiasm, Jericho was quick to agree that Maria had chosen well when she left the renovations and refurbishing of her newly acquired home to Adams Cade's elegant, talented wife.

The lady knew her stuff. In the bargain, she was a meticulous planner, and an uncanny judge of the time that would be required for each task. Eden worked hard, never sparing herself, within limits dictated by an unexpected condition. She was thoughtful and reasonable and considerate of the needs of the various crews. In return, when she asked for an hour of work, the carpenters, painters, or whoever, gave her the full sixty minutes.

"The lady really could charm birds out of trees."

"Has Maria's extended absence driven you to talking to yourself, Jericho?" Adams Cade fell into step beside him. Dressed in jeans and a flannel shirt to guard against the first hint of autumn's chill, Eden's smiling husband carried a haphazard collection of oversize books in his arms.

"So it would seem," Jericho admitted ruefully. "But I was speaking of Eden. The lady's a magician. From the looks of this place, and with the amount of work your wife can coax out of the crews, Lady's Hall will be ready and as marvelous as Maria Elena hoped. She'll be more than pleased, when she finally comes home."

"Maria's been gone a long time." Detouring, Adams set the books of wallpaper reproductions on a table, then returned to Jericho. The frown that marred his face was rare now, and though there was more silver in his dark brown hair, a look of deep contentment filled Adams's brown eyes. "Longer than you ever expected, I imagine."

"A month became six weeks. Six weeks has become nearly three months." Jericho's shoulder lifted in an unconvincing dismissal. "Maria Elena predicted it might. Anyway, she's called, when she could. And written a few times. Twice to be honest. Each letter took as long as three weeks getting to me."

"It's tough and getting tougher, isn't it? Doesn't matter that you've been in touch, or even that you know she's okay at that given moment. Nothing changes the bottom line,'' Adams commiserated quietly. ''Your lady's in danger, and you're worried.''

''Out of my mind,'' Jericho admitted.

Adams made a sound deep in his throat. He looked beyond the back door toward the docks, where Eden would be. ''I can imagine, my friend,'' he murmured. ''How well I can imagine.''

Following the direction of Adams's attention, Jericho broached the subject that had brought him to Lady's Hall after a long, discouraging day. ''I was wondering if Eden might have heard from her. Maybe last night, or today.''

''Sorry, no,'' Adams said regretfully. ''Nothing in weeks.''

''It's been over two weeks since I heard from her. So I was hoping...'' Jericho stopped short. He hadn't the words to express what he hoped. As he rested a palm at his nape, his craggy face was stark, his handsome mouth grave.

''It's worse than going crazy, isn't it,'' Adams said, rather than asked. ''Twists your gut and hurts like hell.''

''Yeah.'' Jericho nodded. ''Like hell, but worse.''

Adams smiled wryly, but his eyes were grave as he clasped his tall friend on the shoulder. ''I never thought I would see either of us in this circumstance. The outcast of the Cades and Belle Terre's eternally elusive bachelor worrying over the only women either of us has ever loved. It might be funny at times, if it weren't for the fact that it hurts so much at others.''

''Funny? Yeah,'' Jericho said in an undertone. ''At times.''

While they talked, Jericho and Adams walked through the house. Now, when they stepped onto the back veranda, Eden came into view. As she moved purposely about the dock, it was an easy thing to imagine that this was how Maria would look, tending her project, carrying a baby inside her. His child. As Eden carried Adams's child.

The image eased the ache in Jericho's heart, if only for a moment. A child with Maria? Perhaps another little girl. One who would live and grow strong, and be cherished enough for two. The idea had occurred to him before, but he'd never dared admit even to himself how badly he wanted a family with Maria. Could it be? Ever?

"Adams?" He waited until the man at his side tore his tender regard from his wife. In an unplanned digression rather than the question he'd intended, he said, "The honeymoon isn't over, is it?"

Adams didn't answer immediately. His look strayed again to the dock. In that magical awareness of lovers, Eden paused, glanced up from the task she was supervising, and waved to him. A smile touched Adams's lips and glittering eyes. Softly he said, "Never."

Watching them, Jericho knew this was what he wanted. God willing, he would have it. Someday. "Did you expect all that's happened?" he wondered aloud. "Before you came back to Belle Terre, did you believe it was possible?"

"That I would have Eden and soon a baby?" Adams crossed his arms over his chest as he watched his wife instruct a carpenter on the final repairs the dock for Lady's Hall needed. "Never."

"Only a fool would think you miss prison, but what about the rest, Adams? You were the first wonder of the business world for a time. You could reclaim the title, if you wanted it again."

"I don't miss it. I never wanted the notoriety, Jericho. Other than the day Eden and I were married, three of the best times of my life were when my brother Jefferson was exonerated of any charges in the incident that wrongfully sent me to prison, the day my pardon was granted, and when my brothers and I sold Cade Enterprises, lock, stock, and barrel, to Jacob Helms. Then everything fell into place. I could come home for real and forever, to this."

"We were fortunate in that situation, Adams. Junior Rabb incriminated himself. Pieced together, his ravings told a tale of self-defense on both your part and Jefferson's. Then, not caring a whit for the immunity he was granted, Hobie Verey came forward proving the timetable and making sense of Rabb's drunken babble.''

Jericho watched as Eden crossed the lawn, a smile meant only for Adams on her lovely face. ''In little more than a year your life has come to this. Now all truly is well that ends well.''

Eden's time was near, though she carried her baby low and small. Jericho knew Adams's concern in that, especially with a babe it was feared Eden might never conceive. But the doctor assured them it happened sometimes, and that full-term babies carried small were as healthy and no less a happy miracle.

''It won't be long now,'' Jericho said with a small, crooked smile. ''Then the Cades will celebrate another best day.''

''A Christmas baby, if she cooperates. That's why Eden put on extra crews, hoping the house would be completed by the holidays. Instead, here we are finishing weeks ahead of schedule. If she were here, Maria could move in when the painters and paperhangers finish the foyer.'' Adams flashed Jericho a grin. ''Of course, Eden has a cleanup crew waiting in the wings.''

''Eden would.'' Jericho expected no less. ''Then, thanks to your amazing, efficient wife, to you, and to Cullen, of course, all that will be needed for the project to be complete is Maria Elena.''

''I came home, Jericho,'' Adams reminded quietly. ''One day, Maria will, too.''

Jericho crossed his arms over his chest. Unlike Adams he wore only his uniform. His shirt was khaki, not flannel. He'd been so hopeful for news Eden might have of Maria, he'd come straight to Lady's Hall from his duties. Thus, he hadn't changed. A windbreaker lay in the car, but his need wasn't that great. Not for a jacket.

''Maybe you're right, Adams,'' he murmured. ''Maybe Maria Elena will come home. One day.''

"How about now?"

Certain he was hallucinating, Jericho spun about, his mouth dry, his heart pounding. The vision he encountered was a woman dressed in the heavy, masculine clothing of war, a bulky bag of camera equipment sliding from her shoulder to the floor. He knew. There was never any doubt in his mind or his heart. Still, in his shock, he whispered, "Maria? Maria Elena?"

"Maria Elena Rivers to be exact." She was pale and haggard as she stood at the edge of the veranda. When he took a lurching step, reaching out to take her in his arms, against his shoulder she whispered, "Hold me, Jericho. I think that if you don't, I shall surely collapse at your feet."

"Are you hurt?" he growled desperately into her hair.

"Just tired." She nestled against him, letting him take her slight weight. "So tired. Just hold me. That's all I need."

Jericho wanted to look at her, to run his searching gaze over her, to discover the truth for himself. Yet he couldn't bear to let her go. Instead, oblivious of Adams and Eden, carpenters and paperhangers, on the veranda of Lady's Hall he held her, rocking her in his embrace.

Stroking her hair, he murmured to her, at first not really caring if his words made sense, only that they soothed her, comforted her. Then he realized Adams was touching his shoulder in a silent offer of help. Jericho only shook his head, never breaking the soft, chanting cadence of words of assurance and love.

"She's exhausted," he said at last over Maria's head, as Eden joined them with a solemn look of distress.

"Would you like to take her to the inn? Or the river cottage?" Eden asked. "It's practically next door. Cullen could draw her a hot bath, bring a bottle of brandy…"

"No!" In his disquiet Jericho spoke more harshly than he intended. "I'm sorry, Eden, I didn't mean to be abrupt. I appreciate your kind offer and hospitality, but I'm taking Maria Elena home."

Lifting her into his arms, his lips brushed her temple as he whispered a question, "My home, just for now, dear heart?"

"Yes, please." Her voice was low, ragged. Her clasp at his neck was tight and trembling from bone-deep fatigue. But even more from the horror of all she'd seen.

When Maria buried her face in the curve of his throat, Jericho met the compassionate gazes of Adams and Eden, and nodded his goodbye. As he turned from them to retrace his steps through Lady's Hall and then to his car, he knew no words were necessary. He'd read in Adams's face, and in Eden's, that they understood this paramount need to be together and alone.

Jericho knew, without the words, that should any difficulty arise, these good, caring friends were only a phone call away.

She was shivering by the time he parked the car in his drive. Though the autumn air felt cooler than the temperature would merit were it not for the humidity, it still shouldn't warrant shivering. Yet when he crossed to the passenger's side to help her from the car, her hands were cold, her skin tinged with blue.

"We're home, Maria Elena," he murmured as he stepped with her through his front door. Now that he was calmer, he was painfully aware that she was thinner, perhaps even ill. "There'll be a warm bath waiting for you by the time we discard this clothing, I promise."

Jericho's home was a bachelor's home, suited for a large and virile man. Everything within its walls had been planned to accommodate his size. The rooms, the chairs, his bed, his bath, and the open spaces. The spaciousness and the masculine simplicity only served to enhance a pleasant and restful ambience. And now, with the security he'd added in hopeful anticipation of the day his home would become Maria Elena's home, she would be safe as well as warm and rested, and loved.

"I dreamed of this," Maria spoke as he took her to a chair

in his bedroom. Jericho's bedroom. The room in which they'd made love the night reporting the museum gala brought her back to Belle Terre at last. She hoped they would make love here again. Not this night, her mind was too filled with chaos, her body too battered. But soon they would be lovers again.

"While I was in the desert, when it was so cold in the night, I would think of this room, with the warm sun streaming through the open doors." Jericho knelt before her, and now she stroked his cheek, proving he wasn't a dream. "I pretended I was here with you, Jericho, warmed by the sun, by your arms. By your touch."

Her words were hesitant and thick from fatigue and God only knew what else. Jericho was seized by a killing rage directed at a man she'd spoken of in her calls. A man he didn't know and had never seen. Rage he barely restrained as he finished taking off her boots and heavy socks, then helped her to her bare feet.

"You were cold in the desert." His words were bitter with his fury. "Does that mean you were in the desert when you were with this Josef and his rebel band?"

Maria made a hoarse sound of assent as he slid her field jacket from her shoulders and began to deal with the metal buttons of her shirt. One by one they slipped free of the coarse, sturdy fabric. Inch by inch her shirt opened. She meant to stop him, for she didn't want him to see her as she was—bruised, scrawny. With the taint of a vicious, despicable war of genocide still clinging to her like a sordid memory.

In desperation to be done with the hatefulness and the horror of her assignment, in her thoughtless, headlong flight from it, she hadn't considered its repercussions. She hadn't considered how she might feel, or look. Maria hadn't considered anything except her need for Jericho.

Standing in his softly lit bedroom, she felt undeserving of the warmth, the serenity, and his gentle kindness. Yet the brush of his knuckles against her breasts as he made careful work of buttons was too soothing, too comforting for guilt. As she fell beneath the spell only Jericho could weave with a touch, she couldn't muster the will to rebuff his tender ministrations.

In her heart, despite the anguish of her newly disturbed conscience, she knew she didn't want him to stop. Not now. Not ever.

Instead, as the weariness seemed to ascend tenfold, she stood obediently beneath his riveted attention as he dealt in watchful deference with her clothing. He seemed to understand that even the slide of rough fabric across her skin was an exquisite ache. Jericho seemed to understand everything.

Her shirt and the restraining undergarments she wore beneath it were gone. With the kiss of his warm breath on the chafed and tender skin of her breasts, Maria sighed softly, her body longing for more even in the throes of mental turmoil.

Intent on his task, for Jericho the low, hoarse sound was a measure of her fatigue. Kneeling before her again, he dealt with the baggy, heavy trousers. Clothing she hadn't bothered to change in her haste to board the military plane that had been sent for her. As carefully as before, Jericho slipped the mesh belt from its loops and, more quickly, dispatched the button at her waist. With the growl of a zipper he was drawing the last of the garments of war from his lady warrior.

He touched her and held her as if she would break. As if even the trace of his gaze would hurt. Maria had known such exquisite tenderness only once before. Only with the young, gallant Jericho. She knew now they had been too young then. Too new to love. In the measure of years, they had been little more than children, making the mistakes of untried youth.

But even in his youthfulness, this gentle giant called Jericho would have made a good father. As she watched, in her mind, in her heart, Maria could see how he would've been with a little girl. She could imagine their little girl with sparkling gray eyes, watching as she had watched, while his big fingers struggling in clumsy care with tiny buttons as he readied her for a bath.

Tears flooded Maria's eyes, and her slight shudder coincided with the slow slide of the last of her clothing from her body. Misunderstanding, because he couldn't know the direction of her thoughts, Jericho whispered, "Sorry, love. I know you're cold. Just this little bit and the task will be done."

True to his word, before she realized, she was naked and he was taking her in his arms again. Only then did she know he'd divested himself of his shirt. With the delicious scent of Jericho filling her lungs and the taste of him on her lips, she protested, "I can walk, you know. If I managed to get to Lady's Hall from the other side of the world, I can manage your bathroom."

"Of course you can." He made no move to set her down. "But I'm here, now, and you don't have to manage anything."

"Jericho..." Whatever she would have said was forgotten as he stopped in the midpoint of the hall. Gathering her even closer, he stared down at her without speaking. In his face she saw grief. In his eyes, unfathomable hurt.

"I had to let you walk away from me and into danger, because I hadn't the right to ask you not to go," he said at last. "While you were gone, I was demented with worry. Now you're home after too long, and *I* need this. I need to take care of you, Maria Elena. Like I've never needed anything before."

Tears threatened again, but she fought them back. When he explained it so tenderly, she would have allowed him anything. "I'm sorry. I didn't understand."

"Shh. No, love. No apologies between us."

His look held Maria's until she stroked his cheek and agreed. "No apologies."

He took her then to a part of his house she'd never seen. Beyond a door leading from the master bath with its basic furnishings and customary spacious design, lay a solarium of two stories that was anything but basic. With ceilings and walls of glass, for her pleasure it offered the sky for her perusal, an overlook of an extraordinary stretch of marsh, then, in the distance, the river that formed the estuary. With thriving coastal trees and plants scattered around the interior, a breeze was all Maria needed to think Jericho had stepped outside.

But the outside would be cool and growing dark. Here there was soft light and heat. Even with the small pool that beckoned like an oasis, one wouldn't mistake it for the wilds of the South Carolina Low Country.

As Jericho descended the open stairs and passed before a wall of mirrors, through the fleeting glimpses of burning eyes, she realized he'd removed more than his shirt and shoes. Wearing only briefs, a second later he stepped with her into the heated, turbulent water of the pool.

As he settled her before him on a low banquette, the churning heat reached into her, finding each taut, tired muscle, each sore tendon. With swirling ripples teasing over her skin, enticing her to relax, Maria sighed and leaned into his embrace.

The water, the heat, and Jericho's arms were like a drug, seducing her into oblivion. Oblivion without suffering, without guilt, without fear. For the first time in nearly three months, she didn't feel the burden of tragedy. For the first time since she left Belle Terre and Jericho, Maria didn't dread the night.

He knew when she relaxed. So attuned was he to every nuance of her body, Jericho knew when she succumbed to the first stage of sleep. Patiently he waited until her sleep was deep. Then, turning her in his arms, he bathed her, cursing only in his mind over scrapes and bruises of varying degrees. He wouldn't question Maria, but he would have answers from Simon for some of her hurts.

When he'd finished, he stepped from the pool, bearing her weight gently. He didn't dry her. Instead, leaving her to sleep the deep, precious sleep, he wrapped her in a warmed towel. Dimming the lights even more and cradling her against him, he sat with her before the windows watching the marsh at night.

* * *

In the small hours of the morning he took her to his bed.
She'd slept for hours in his arms, and still she didn't rouse.

"So tired," he murmured as he coiled a dark strand of her
hair around his palm, then let it drift to the pillow. He intended
to join her, just to hold her, when he was startled by the sound
of a car moving stealthily down his drive. Assaulted by memories
of the last unannounced visitor bringing news of a
bombed and burning car, every nerve was alert and jangling.

Taking jeans and a shirt from a closet, he slipped into them,
then slid bare feet into moccasins. As he dressed, he paused
to listen again. The car moved furtively, headlights dark. It
wouldn't be Court or any of his deputies. None of them would
worry about waking him, since that would be the primary intent
if any of his staff were coming to his house.

"But they wouldn't come. They would call," he muttered,
recalling the morning Court had come to his house and awakened
him. But only because he'd turned off his phone.

Whoever traversed his drive so cautiously certainly didn't
have waking the house in mind. Not for a while.

Lovers? Jericho wondered as he strapped on his holster and
slid his weapon home. It was unlikely the kids of Belle Terre
would make out in the sheriff's drive. Yet, while he doubted
he would find some jock and a cheerleader or a couple of class
brains in the back seat of a hot rod, stranger things had happened.

Silently crossing to the door, he paused, wondering if he
should wake Maria. Then, on second thought, he discarded the
idea. This could be a false alarm, and she was in desperate
need of rest.

Slipping out the door to the hall, he descended the stairs.
Keeping to the shadows and beyond the light of a harvest
moon, he moved like a ghost to a side door obscured by a
thick bed of plants. In minutes, he'd circled the house, insuring
that if intrusion were the intent, it wouldn't be twofold, with
one from the marsh or the estuary, as well.

Blackly green in early moonlight, marsh grass stood undisturbed by human trespass. The estuary and the shore were as quiet as either could be with night creatures moving about. All Jericho need concern himself with was the vehicle drawing to a halt by his door. The car was a Jaguar, black, gleaming, powerful. Not what the average thief, bomber, or teenage Lothario would drive. But its headlights were still dark, not the way the average honest citizen would drive in the wee hours.

While Jericho watched from the cover of a lush grove of palmettos, a man of no little size, with shoulders like a bull, opened the driver's door. Interior lights proved he was alone. Unless, Jericho thought, accomplices crouched in hiding.

As if his size were nothing, the intruder moved agilely. Rather than stealth, Jericho sensed care. Whoever he was, whatever he wanted, this man of bull shoulders and hidden features didn't wish to disturb the house.

None of it made sense, until the intruder moved past the coach lamp. Caught in the light that marked the path to the front door, craggy features leaped familiarly from beneath a thatch of distinctive silver-dusted hair cut short.

"Simon?" Hardly believing what he saw, Jericho stepped into the circle of light, his hand hovering over his weapon. "What the hell are you doing creeping down my drive at this ungodly hour?"

Despite Jericho's harsh tone, the reply was unruffled. "I came to see about Maria. If she was sleeping, I didn't want to wake her."

"You flew from Washington at this hour to see Maria?" If so, then he would have rented the car.

"Actually, no." Simon McKinzie's answer was less a whisper than a low growl. "I drove from my home in the mountains."

Jericho knew there was such a place. A place called by many names among the few he knew who worked for the wily Scot. Simon's lair. Simon's retreat. Simon's refuge. Even Simon's den. Jericho didn't know its true name or the exact location of the fabled sanctuary, but he knew the approximate area. If one could call the range of the Blue Ridge Mountains an approximation.

"I don't suppose Jaguars are the fashion in rentals. At least it wouldn't be wise around here," Jericho said bitterly.

"With the bomber still about, you mean?"

Of course Simon would know. He would make it his business to know everything about his agents. And Yancey Hamilton had sent specimens and any other information he could gather to Simon's experts. "Is there something new on the bomb? Is that another reason you're here?"

Simon shook his leonine head. "My people haven't turned up any more than Yancey. I didn't expect they would or could. If Yancey can't find the key, nobody can."

"I know how good he is." With a resigned look, Jericho gestured Simon toward the front door. "If we're going to have the talk we both know is coming, we might as well do it inside. Maria's sleeping upstairs—I could probably make some coffee or pour a drink or two without waking her." With a rueful smile he added, "Frankly, I suspect I could run a flock of squawking blue herons through and she wouldn't wake."

"She's that tired?" Simon asked, his voice expressing the concern mirrored on his face.

"She's that tired, and worse." Jericho stepped aside for the older man to precede him. Shutting the door behind them, he let the latch click quietly back into place.

"Now, why don't you tell me why you've come to see about Maria Elena? And how the hell you knew she would be with me." Jericho set a tall Scotch before the Scot and settled in a chair across from him. Setting his own drink aside, he folded his hands and didn't touch the glass again as he waited for Simon's response.

"To answer your questions, I came because I know my people." Simon faced the light, his strong features a mass of shadows and lines. But the jut of his chin and the steady regard

of his hooded eyes, unmistakable Simon McKinzie trade-
marks, were clearly visible. The attitude of the first, and the
look in the second, spoke of more than mere concern. "I know
what they can do. I know their breaking points, and what can
trigger them. I know why.

"I knew Maria would be with you because I'm neither deaf
nor blind. And because one and one still make two. I reached
that sum the first time you worked with The Watch. The sheriff of Belle Terre, a dedicated bachelor, wore a gold band on
his right hand. One of my better agents wears an identical band
on a bangle welded around her wrist. He's originally from
Belle Terre. She's originally from Belle Terre, and of the same
age. Or almost."

Simon paused, fixing his piercing gaze on Jericho. "Do I
have to explain that the rest was pure deduction?"

"In other words—" Jericho laughed with a wry tone
"—you didn't have a shred of real fact as basis for this pure
deduction until now."

"Sometimes a hunch and a sure thing are one and the same.
All either needs is the final proof."

"It was you who got her out of Belle Terre to give the rest
of us time to resolve this bombing incident, wasn't it,
Simon?" Jericho was playing his own hunch-cum-sure-thing.
"Then when the mission went wrong, it was you who resolved
the situation and sent the plane for her."

Simon didn't bother to deny Jericho's logic. "We needed
her. That was no ploy. She knew Josef. He trusted her and
listened to her before. I thought he would again."

Simon paused, his massive hand curled tautly around his
glass of Scotch. "What I didn't count on was that his own
son would betray him for the traitor's thirty pieces of silver."

"An act that left me in the hands of a band of rebels reduced
to rabble without Josef's powerful magnetism and stern lead-
ership."

Simon and Jericho both turned to the door where Maria
stood. In the faint light she should have seemed fragile and

lost in the folds of Jericho's robe—instead she was magnificent.

As both men leaped to their feet, Simon was first to break a silence that spun into tense seconds. "An unforgivable ignorance, Maria," he confessed. "For that I will be eternally sorry."

"How could you know, Simon," she asked softly, with no rancor in her voice, "when his own father didn't?"

Simon heard forgiveness in her words. He nodded, his eyes still shadowed with regret. "My report said your physical injuries weren't serious."

"You sent the best of The Watch after me. Then provided an escort to insure my safe return. Yet you had to see for yourself," she suggested quietly. "Now you have."

"Will you be all right, truly?" Simon's gaze bored into hers, seeking his own answer, his own truth.

Leaving the doorway, Maria crossed to Jericho. When she paused beside him, as if it were only natural, as if she were a necessary part of him, he drew her close. Sheltered beneath his arm, comforted by the strength he lent to her own, Maria looked into the probing stare of one of the world's most private and most powerful men.

"I'll be fine now, Simon." Her fingers closed over Jericho's hands, and she was comforted again by his unfaltering devotion as he completed the circle of the haven of his arms. With a slow smile and renewed confidence, Maria said, "Truly, I will."

Eight

The view from the solarium was mesmerizing. Drops of moisture collecting on slender stalks of marsh grass reflected the first spark of the sun in a glitter of rainbows. Beyond the marsh the wide, curving river captured the color of the sky, turning its placidly flowing water to liquid turquoise. Close by the house, barely stirring palms and palmettos shivered beneath the brush of a subtle breeze and whispered a lazy reply.

The morning couldn't have been more beautiful, or more inviting, but Jericho was scarcely aware of the world beyond the glass. It was the woman nearly lost in one of his shirts who captured his attention. It was she who mesmerized him as she watched the beginning of the day in childlike fascination.

Maria hadn't looked away from the view when Jericho descended the spiral stair. She didn't turn or speak when he came silently to her, his hand at her midriff drawing her back against his bare chest. In her heart she saw him as she'd left him at dawn, his black hair tousled, his expression solemn in sleep but content.

As she'd watched him in first light, she'd ached to return to his bed. Ached for him to take her in his arms, holding her close as he had in the night. So close the beat of two hearts would be as one, the shared warmth one warmth. The love one love. Then, perhaps, the shadows of misgiving lurking in the back of her mind, driving her away from Jericho and Belle Terre, might be banished forever.

But she hadn't returned to his bed. She hadn't sought solace in his arms. Instead she'd wandered to the solarium to think. To find a way for dreams she'd never dared to dream would come true.

"I never imagined it could be like this," she whispered, as if the sound of her voice could shatter a perfect moment, bringing the truth tumbling down around them.

"You've seen the sun on the marshes many times, Maria Elena," he said quietly, his lips touching the curve of her throat.

"Not in a long, long while." Crossing her arms over his, determined not to let disquieting concerns destroy this day, Maria leaned her head against his shoulder. "Never with you, like this."

"No." He held her tighter. "Never like this." For Jericho, the night and this day were a gift, a time he never expected. One he hoped was the prophesy for the rest of their lives.

More than twenty-four hours had passed since he'd sat quietly in the predawn hours, listening as she spoke with Simon. As he heard what was a carefully gentle debriefing by the venerable leader of The Black Watch, Jericho discovered a woman of abiding strengths and remarkable wisdom. He knew then that whatever the trials Maria suffered in the hands of Josef's rabble band, she had grown stronger. She had grown wiser.

He'd seen clearly then that the wounds of mind and heart and body would heal. The exhaustion would pass. The woman who survived, the woman who would do what she must no matter the danger or the hurt, would be more. Never less.

Was this the rare quality Simon McKinzie saw in those he called his chosen? If so, where did it come from, this caring, this giving, this courage? Where? Jericho wondered as he kissed Maria's temple, letting his lips follow a tracery of pale blue veins.

Simon claimed he knew his people. That he knew their strengths, their weaknesses, their breaking points. That he knew why. Jericho believed every word. He'd no doubt the shrewd Scot had tested and would test, again and again, every strength and every weakness of each of his people.

Yet Simon worried, and he cared. Tough, demanding, and relentless, Simon cared so deeply, he couldn't stay away. Though he'd needed to see for himself about Maria, Jericho had come to realize the Scot recognized something in her he hadn't. It took Simon to show him Maria would be stronger for the hardship, for the pain.

But strong, or not, Jericho could not quell a deep-seated resentment that Simon had set Maria in the path of danger.

"Are you truly all right?" He'd heard her say she was in the discussion with Simon. He needed to hear it now, meant only for him.

"I'm better than all right, Jericho," Maria assured him, her voice like gentle music as she set aside her worries. Working for Simon, even a short time, had taught her the value of each moment, each day. This day with Jericho she would treasure.

As his arms fell away, she faced him, her gray gaze calm and steady. "The situation in the desert was worse than unpleasant, but I was never truly in danger. Josef's son might betray his father, but he would never hurt me. He saw me as a pipeline, the voice to speak his words to the world. My survival was his top priority."

Her lips tilted in satisfaction. "Holding me prisoner will mean his downfall that much sooner. Simon will see to it."

"And I would help Simon. Dammit Maria Elena! You were

bruised, battered, and beyond exhaustion.'' Jericho stopped short, his expression grim. ''I saw horror in your eyes.''

''Perhaps. But, darling, what a mission takes from us, in the long run, it gives back in renewed strength, in a sense of contribution and accomplishment. In lessons learned.''

Jericho barely heard her, for in all their short times together, Maria rarely spoke an endearment. He wanted to hear it again. Instead he sought reassurance. ''You truly feel rested.''

Maria laughed huskily then. ''I should be, considering.''

Jericho smiled at the emphasis, for it was her rueful reminder that even after Simon was satisfied and took his leave of them, Maria was restless and moody. Until she'd enticed him to his own bed and made love to him with a fierceness that spoke of driving out the last demon. Then, exhausted in mind and body, but with a calmed heart, she'd slept. For twenty-four hours, she slept and barely moved. And, never leaving her side, Jericho kept his vigil.

When he slept, at last, then woke with a new dawn to find her missing, he knew where he would find her. As he'd slipped into a pair of slacks then wandered to the solarium in his bare feet, he hadn't stopped to wonder how he knew, he simply accepted that he did.

''You never doubted I would be here?'' she asked.

''Never.''

Maria nodded, and nothing more was needed. Wrapped in his arms, she watched the awakening of a world far removed, and yet strangely similar to the world she'd recently departed.

A flock of egrets circled the marsh, white feathers creamy in the sunrise. A solitary great blue, the largest of the Low Country herons, stalked the estuary in solemn majesty. Perched on a stalk of marsh grass barely stirring beneath his weight, a red-winged blackbird sang to the morning.

It was an idyllic panorama, almost seducing one into believing the rest of the world was as idyllic. But amid hope, there were troubles to resolve. Jericho had lived long and hard enough to know what one wanted wasn't always what was best for another.

As if she were attuned to his thoughts, Maria sought the comfort of his embrace. With her face tilted toward his and her dark hair tumbling down her back to brush his wrist, she murmured, "I wish we could stay forever in this small haven."

As she stroked his face, Jericho turned his lips into her palm, leaving a kiss in its hollow. "But we can't. So what do we do?"

Sliding her hands from his face, over his shoulders, then his arms, she loosed herself from him. Stepping away, because she couldn't think when he touched her or kissed her, she stood apart. "I'm not sure." Softly, she added, "I didn't expect this."

She was a pale shape against the light of the sun as it lifted over a grove of trees and blazed unfettered into the solarium. Only a fascinating silhouette with the wild cascade of her hair giving back the light in dark fire. Even in shadow she was beautiful in the eyes of a man who loved her. A man who had loved her more than half his life.

Reading wonder and troubled concern in her voice, Jericho waited, saying nothing.

"When the assignment to cover the museum opening crossed my desk, I was determined to refuse it. Then, when I stopped to think and let myself feel, I knew I wanted to come."

"Why?" he asked as quietly as she'd spoken.

"I wanted to see you, Jericho."

"What didn't you expect?"

She hesitate, drawing a long, shuddering breath. "That you wouldn't hate me. That my dreams were real and you were as I remembered. That I would love the man the Jericho of my memory had become." Her face was still in shadow, but he felt her seeking gaze, as she whispered, "That I would never want to leave you."

"But...?" he continued for her, needing to hear the rest.

"But," she murmured. "A small word encompassing problems."

"I love you, Maria Elena. I tried not to love you after you left. I took off your ring and did my best to go on with my life. It didn't work. You were too much a part of me. We belonged together. If not here, then somewhere else."

She stepped closer, her face illuminated now by a shaft of light. "You would leave Belle Terre?"

"I would have left Belle Terre years ago, if you'd asked."

Silence hung in sunlight like a vacuum. Maria turned her gaze from Jericho's, her face solemn. "It wouldn't have worked. I was too confused, too hurt. Too bitter. In my mind, you were one of *them*. Even worse, you were a Rivers, one of the elite of Belle Terre. I was a Delacroix." She broke off, unable to relive the degradation.

"I didn't give a damn what your name was," Jericho said hoarsely. "I didn't give a damn who your father was, or wasn't. Or your grandmother. Or the grandmother before her."

"I know that now. I think I knew it then. But I was afraid," she whispered. "Afraid of my own instincts. Afraid to believe in you. More than anything I was afraid that, in time, the kindness and the love would die. Then we would be simply a Rivers and a Delacroix, caught in the trap of marriage."

"If it was a trap, it was one neither of us ever bothered with the smallest effort to escape, Maria Elena."

"I thought *you* would need to escape. For years I waited for a letter saying you wanted out. I believed it for a long time. The night of the museum gala, I was shaking in fear that it would finally be true. But I was determined I wouldn't let it hurt." Taking another step toward him, she touched his hair, his face, letting her fingertips linger at his lips.

"Then, in the moonlight, you came to me, taking me in your arms. And I was lost again. You could have tormented me for what I'd done those long years ago. But one look in your eyes and I knew. Jericho Rivers still wanted me, at least for the moment, and he would never hurt me.''

Hurt her? He would die first. Want her? Jericho wondered if there had been a day he hadn't missed her, hadn't wanted her. He wanted her now and forever. If forever could be theirs.

Into his silent thoughts, she recounted, ''You never hurt me, you never questioned. In the greatest test of trust, when Simon called, you didn't try to keep me.''

''If you love a woman,'' Jericho paraphrased, ''let her go.''

''And she will come back to you,'' Maria finished for him. ''Thank God this time didn't take so long.''

Jericho laughed ruefully. ''Speak for yourself, sweetheart. I could have sworn the last three months were eighteen years.''

''I didn't mean to worry you.''

''You were doing your job,'' he said before the next apology. ''And you did warn me. Three damned months.''

How much didn't he know of those months? Jericho wondered. Even with her solemn assurances, she'd told him very little. As she'd told him little of the weeks, months, and years after she'd left him. ''They couldn't have been easy.''

''I've been through worse, and been treated worse, Jericho. But I've never seen worse conditions.''

She thought he spoke of the present, of the mission for The Black Watch. Jericho didn't correct her. There would be time later to delve into the past. Now, Maria needed to address a more recent past. As much as she would, or could.

''I know it's happened time and again, but I'd never witnessed prejudice and hatred that teetered on the brink of war and genocide. In Josef's country, I saw children starving. Why? For what reason?'' she spat. ''Bigotry, fear, sheer malice. For the color of their eyes and their skin, or for what their parents believed.

''In a small, less malignant way, Belle Terre is guilty of the same sin of pride and cruel judgment.''

''As you were judged.'' Anger colored Jericho's words. For the child they'd lost to that cruel judgment. For the years.

Maria turned to the window, pacing restlessly before it, the pain of old wounds suddenly too much to face.

Jericho knew where her thoughts had gone. He recognized the bleak look, the sense of helplessness, the restlessness. He'd been there many times.

Morning was in full swing, the sun was bright, and the breeze had dwindled. The day would be warming. He offered a diversion. "It's a beautiful morning, let's enjoy it while it lasts. But first, are you hungry, Maria Elena? Would you like breakfast?"

In a tilt of her head she refused, never looking away from the marsh and the day.

"Then how about a walk on the beach?" She'd loved the shore as a girl. He suggested it now, remembering that walking in the lazy eddy of the waves always soothed her girlhood hurts.

With a forced laugh, she gestured toward the shirt covering her like a tent. The hem drifted long past mid-thigh, leaving a tempting bit of her legs and ankles exposed. "I doubt my costume would be considered *comme il faut* for your beach."

"It is my beach, and private, within reason. You would look fetching walking my land, wearing my shirt." His laugh was only a little less tense then Maria's. "If you wouldn't be comfortable, I can gather together a beachcomber's costume for you."

"Something that belongs to a lady friend?" Maria's heart plummeted at the thought of another woman with Jericho, perhaps wearing his shirt as she did now, leaving her own. But she hadn't the right to care, and the second the words were out of her mouth, she regretted them. Jericho had said there was no one serious in his life. But if there was someone not so serious, it was none of her business. "I'm sorry, I shouldn't have said that."

"Why shouldn't you?" He crossed to a closet hidden by a wall of mirrors. Hangers clattered as he shuffled through a number of casual garments that were painfully and obviously feminine.

"It was uncalled for and presumptuous."

But Jericho wasn't listening as he considered the contents of the closet. "As a matter of fact, the clothing I have here does belong to a lady friend. A very special lady friend."

"Then maybe I shouldn't…"

"Shouldn't wear them?" There was something wicked about his grin as he faced her, a pair of slacks and a blouse draped over his arm. "Why not? I assure you, my mother won't mind."

"Your mother?"

"Mmm-hmm." He nodded. "She suffers from a mild form of arthritis. Sometimes she comes to soak in the pool. Naturally, she keeps several changes of clothes here."

"Naturally." Maria knew it was selfish to be glad Jericho had no casual relationships, but she couldn't quite subdue a smile.

"In return, in unnecessary but welcome repayment for the use of my pool, she leaves a stock of her sugar cookies."

"Sugar cookies?" Maria chuckled. The thought of this great, handsome giant with a sugar cookie clutched in his hand was too wonderful. The chuckle became laughter. "Sugar cookies!"

"Best in the state," Jericho said pleasantly, without apology. "Best in the world, my grandmother's recipe."

Maria sobered. "I met your mother and your grandmother, once. After a late lesson at Lady Mary's. They were gracious."

"They still are. Grace is their nature. Even though Mother's a Yankee, and *Grandmère* is still a firebrand—whose exact age remains a not-so-well guarded secret." Jericho offered a pair of slacks that would be only a little too large. Apparently his mother was still trim. "Mother's taste doesn't run to sweatshirts, but I have one that should do nicely."

"I could wear it for a gown, you mean." The grin she tossed him was saucy, with worry tucked out of sight.

"Sorry. It's just your bad luck that you fell in love with a small giant." Ruffling her hair, letting it slide like black silk between his fingers as he'd wanted to all morning, he kissed her quickly. "Get dressed. I'll grab a couple of sweatshirts and meet you on the veranda. First one there gets another kiss."

Jericho was first, of course. And of course when she rose on tiptoe to pay her dues, he swept her close in a hard embrace, muttering, "I'd forgotten what a little thing you are."

"Jericho." Maria laughed as her ribs were nearly crushed. "Except for Cullen, everyone is a little thing compared to you."

"You've lost weight," he said as if it were a crime.

"It happens on assignments." She shrugged away the loss.

"Especially assignments like this one," he almost snarled.

"It's over." Backing out of his fierce clasp, she looped an arm through his. "Let's forget about it and just walk."

"First this." As if she were fragile, he dressed her in a tattered sweatshirt bearing the logo of the pro football team for which he'd played. Its sleeves fell beyond her fingertips, the banded bottom skimmed across her knees. Laughing, he murmured, "You look like an orphan. A bewitching orphan."

The shirt enveloped her in the clean, masculine scent of Jericho, fresh air, and the sea. Drawing in the comforting, heart-healing balm, savoring the memories it stirred, she asked softly, "If I were an orphan, would you take me in?"

"In a heartbeat." Casting an arm around her shoulder, he tucked her against him. Smiling down at her, he dropped a kiss on her forehead. "I would hope forever."

Before Maria could think or respond, he whisked her across the veranda, down the steps to the boardwalk, and the shore.

"I'd almost forgotten this, too." Maria walked at the water's edge, her bare feet sinking in damp sand, her hands in the pockets of borrowed slacks. The laces of a pair of sneakers she'd taken the liberty of confiscating from the solarium closet were tied and tossed across her shoulder. With each step one worn shoe brushed against her back, the other against an unbound breast.

Jericho had trudged beside her for longer than an hour. Conversing in short comments or questions when Maria wished, on whatever topic she wished. Then, just as easily, falling into a companionable silence when she was silent. Now he asked, thoughtfully, "What had you forgotten, love?"

"Days like this, when autumn's almost at an end, with winter poised and waiting. When the air nips at cheeks and bare toes, but it really isn't so cold. I'd forgotten the winter color of the sea, and the restlessness that seems to lie in wait for the first northeaster." Laughing, she slipped her hands from her pockets. "Listen to me, waxing poetic over the harbinger of bad weather."

Capturing her hand in his, Jericho climbed a small hummock that rose above the shore, affording an unfettered view of the marsh, the estuary, and the sea at high tide. An ancient Adirondack chair sat hunkered deeply in drifted sand. Its green paint was mostly peeled away, exposed wood had weathered to silvery gray.

When he sat down as if he knew how to avoid every splinter, then drew her to his lap, Maria knew this was his place. Jericho's special haven. Perhaps where he came to find solace, escaping the rigors of his job. Perhaps where he forgot, and where he remembered.

Folding his arms around her, Jericho sat in silence, watching the little wind tease her hair and paint a glow of pale pink on her cheeks. He felt the rhythm of her breath and the beat of her heart as if they were his own. He heard her soft purr of contentment. He waited.

Sheltered in his embrace, she was still and quiet for a long while. But Jericho was patient. Then, as he knew it would, a door that had opened only a little opened completely.

"I never thought I would walk the beach with you again." There was a touch of wonder in Maria's voice. As if she still couldn't quite believe. "After I left you, in the beginning when I was so frightened and so terribly alone, I didn't think I would survive or escape the streets of San Francisco, either."

Maria had been on the street. Jericho's blood ran cold. His stomach churned at what that might mean for a naive young girl. A thousand questions leaped into his mind, but he said nothing. He asked nothing. This was Maria's story. She must tell it as she wished.

"Darling, don't be concerned." She stroked his fingers as they convulsed at her revelation. "It wasn't as bad as it sounds. I wasn't living on the street or 'working' it as one might assume a young girl would. I made small silhouettes of tourists, establishing my territory on a corner near a park where artists came to paint. With an easel, some construction paper, some mats and cheap frames, and a sharp pair of scissors, I earned enough to get by."

The danger, and the horror of what might have been, was almost his undoing. Still Jericho only listened.

"Getting off the bus in San Francisco was like stepping into another world. I was unsophisticated, but I knew what risks not to take. I only worked among the artists, and never past dark. As time passed, I made friends with the police officers who patrolled the area. I learned their names, asked about their families, made silhouettes of their children from photos they showed me. It was one of the officers who introduced me to Maxie."

"Maxie?" A gull scooped up a fish from the shallows, then led three other gulls on a squawking chase. Jericho didn't notice. His attention was too riveted on the masculine name.

"Actually, he was Serge Maximillian, but I never heard him called anything but Maxie. His restaurant had begun as Maximillian's Waterfront Café. Eventually, it was just Maxie's

Place. The name is unpretentious, but the café was a mix of elegance and friendly charm. Sounds like a contradiction, but it worked.

"Maxie's regulars came from all walks. I think every dignitary and politician in the city was his friend. When we were introduced, he was looking for something unique, and in keeping with the atmosphere, to offer both his regulars and the tourists as keepsakes. He liked the idea of silhouettes."

"What was he like?" Jericho wasn't sure if he should be grateful to this Maxie person, or jealous.

"Maxie was seventy. His wife of fifty years died shortly before we met. They had no children. Except for the café, his life was empty. I became his pet project. It was at his instigation that I enrolled in college, then the master's program. He helped me get scholarships, and I worked when I could at the café. More for Maxie, and because I wanted to, than for the money."

"He was your mentor, you were his friend and gave his life purpose beyond business," Jericho mused, knowing now that he should be deeply grateful.

"Maxie was more than my mentor. He was the father my own drunken father had never been. Perhaps he was my salvation."

"I'd like to meet Maxie Maximillian. I'd like to thank him for the woman you've become."

Maria grew quiet, her gaze focused on distant waves flashing frothy whitecaps against the horizon. Turning at last, looking into Jericho's eyes, she stroked the line of his stubbled jaw. "I wish you could meet him—you would have liked each other."

Catching a slow breath, she said, "He predicted this time would come for us. When I didn't believe him, Maxie would only smile and say I should wait until the time was right. Then I would see. I wish he could know he was right."

"Maxie died?" Jericho felt her grief and her loss. In a strange way, he knew it was his loss as well.

"Two years ago. One day his kind heart just stopped. He gave me a life, Jericho. He was instrumental in my getting my first job in broadcasting. Then, as if that weren't enough, he left me a fortune."

"What do you consider a fortune, Maria Elena?"

"This." Her answer came quickly. "Sitting here with you. Being held by you. Hearing you say you love me. This is my fortune. A fortune Maxie's millions couldn't buy."

"Maxie's millions." Jericho chuckled, wondering why he wasn't surprised. "It has a nice ring to it."

"There's a nice number attached to it, too."

"You have millions, yet your lifestyle hasn't changed?" As Maria settled back against him, Jericho stroked her hair, absently watching the rushing tides of the sea.

"I don't think Maxie expected it would change my life any more than it changed his. After his death, in going through his papers, I discovered I wasn't the only young person he helped."

"So you want to continue as he did?" Jericho ventured a hunch. "Pay back his generosity with more generosity."

"I don't want to rush into anything without giving it a lot of thought and consideration, but whatever I decide, I'd like to think Maxie would approve."

"In the meantime, you intend to keep on as before." The stroke of his hand growing still, Jericho was quiet for a time. In his mind he could easily imagine the friendship of a childless old man and a vibrant young woman determined to make a life for herself. Serge Maximillian would approve of that life, but he would worry. As Jericho had worried.

"How long have you worked for Simon? How did it come to pass?" The Black Watch was the most clandestine of organizations. But in Maria's involvement, secrecy had been breached.

"I don't truly work for Simon." Maria made the expected denial, then explained, "Not on a regular basis. The first time was three years ago, when an obscure rebel leader agreed to speak to the press. But only through me. Strangely, it was someone I'd never met. We think he must have drawn my name out of a hat. When Simon heard of it he approached me, and I agreed to do what he asked. After three weeks of intense training—an abbreviated, compacted version he requires of his agents—I was away.''

''That was the beginning.'' Maria couldn't see his face, but she heard the grave tone of his voice.

''There were more missions, Jericho. This was the fifth.''

''And most dangerous,'' Jericho said harshly.

''It wasn't supposed to be. What happened was beyond predicting. None of it was Simon's fault. There's no one to blame except Josef's son and those who bribed him. It could have happened at any time. It could happen again, or never again.'' Her shoulders lifted in a dismissive shrug. ''Call it luck of the draw.''

''Luck, hell!''

Before he could say more, she turned, facing him squarely. Her breasts were soft and enticing beneath his shirt as they brushed against his chest. Her palm curled over his lips, stopping the outpouring of ill temper. ''Shh, no more. I learned a great deal on this mission, and I came to terms with some important issues.

''But I don't want to talk about them. Not now, Jericho. Not for a while. I'm tired of wasting this day in talk. There's a different language I would speak.''

When she straightened from him and took her hand away, the scowl on Jericho's face was fading. A heated look began to glow in his eyes. ''What language would that be, my love?''

''This language.'' Slipping her hands beneath the band of his shirt, she let her fingers glide over his chest. Teasing flat, male nipples to tiny buds before drifting provocatively to the button of his jeans, she watched as his breath caught and his gaze darkened.

''And this.'' Her mouth grazed over his and lingered. The tip of her tongue teased his lips. Enticing, beguiling, seducing, until with a hoarse groan, his arms slid around her shoulders and beneath her knees. Then, with his massive strength, he was rising and tearing his lips from hers. But only to bury them again in the fragrance of her hair as he took her to his house...and his bed.

Nine

"**S**houldn't you be going along to the station?"

As Jericho walked by her side, Maria wandered through the massive rooms of Lady's Hall, her voice echoing along high ceilings as she spoke. She'd spent a second day cloistered with Jericho, sleeping, making love, and sleeping again. This morning, she'd nearly leaped from his bed, rested, revitalized but disturbingly withdrawn and restless.

Though she'd insisted she wouldn't need him, that surely he had a mountain of work to catch up on, Jericho remained just as insistent that he accompany her for her first tour of Lady's Hall to view Eden's renovations. It should have been a festive excursion...instead she'd grown more restive in his company.

"I've already taken up far too much of your time, Jericho." She needed for him to go. She wanted to think. She must. But when he was so near, it was Jericho who filled her mind and dominated her thoughts. "Before long, someone from your staff will be filing a missing persons report on the elusive sheriff himself.''

"Officer O'Brian knows where I am and that I'm going to be late. She's managed without me for two days,'' he reminded Maria. ''Another half day more won't matter.''

"O'Brian?'' The name caught Maria's interest, jangling her memory. She searched her mind for a familiar female face from the past and drew a blank.

"My secretary, the guardian of the sanctity of my office,'' Jericho explained. ''The name is familiar because when we were kids at the academy, she was a new beat cop. The school was in her district, and Yancey Hamilton was her favorite delinquent.

"Though she lets me think I run the station, it's O'Brian who truly does. With as tight a rein as she did her beat. Nobody will miss me, or know I'm not there. Unless she decides to let them.''

As she recalled the woman, Maria's laugh rippled through the room. Even to her own ears, the sound was forced, unnatural. Yet she didn't doubt Officer O'Brian was more than capable. Nor did she doubt the older woman managed certain aspects of police protocol. But Jericho was no shirker—his would be the ultimate control. He was a man who took his work seriously. Too seriously she'd come to fear, as late as this morning.

Striving to shake off tensions that had lain in wait through the relief of escaping the desert and Josef's son, and the joy of returning to Jericho, she focused on Officer O'Brian. ''What I remember is a stern face hiding the tender heart of a woman who judged us only by our behavior. Never by name, or wealth, or heritage. She was kind to me, and I never knew her first name.''

"Her name is Molly.'' The answer was terse, abrupt. ''But as far as she, or anyone else in Belle Terre is concerned, she's Officer O'Brian. Period. Her job is her life.''

Raking a massive hand across his nape, Jericho's gaze narrowed, turning contemplative. "Now that we have that bit of chitchat behind us, are you going to tell me what's going on in that steel-trap mind of yours?"

"Going on?" Maria glanced away from her inspection of the foyer wallpaper, then returned to it with far more interest than the perfect alignment and design merited. "What could be going on?"

Clasping her shoulders, Jericho turned her to him. Troubled gray eyes studied her face. "You said the trip to the Middle East helped you come to terms with some things—at least that was the gist of what you said. That means you've made some decisions."

He waited for Maria to acknowledge or deny his presumption. When she said nothing and only waited for him to speak again, he made a low sound of frustration. "From the way you're behaving, it's a good bet you're certain I'm not going to like these decisions."

"We'll discuss it later." Lifting her hand to his, she stroked his fingers as they gripped her shoulder. "By now, Officer O'Brian must be ready to send a search party to look for you."

"Dammit, forget O'Brian," Jericho muttered. "The town isn't likely to suffer a crime wave for my absence. But if it does and the city fathers want my badge, they can have it."

"Jericho…"

"No." The rebuke was a sharp report, surprising her. His fingers flexed determinedly over her shoulders, yet his touch was not ungentle. "I'm not going anywhere, Maria Elena. Not anywhere," he repeated. "Until you tell me what today is all about."

"I hoped we could do this later, over a bottle of wine, when things were clearer to me and we were both in an easier frame of mind." Jericho was a gentle stoic who wore an air of utter calm. It was an attitude he'd assumed years ago, as chivalrous men of his intimidating size were prone to do. An attitude that would be quickly abandoned when he was protecting his own. Maria never for a moment questioned that Jericho would think of his estranged wife of eighteen years and his recent lover as one of his own.

"What you mean, Maria Elena, is that you planned to soften me up before you hit me with the bad news." His look was bleak, his face grave. "In that case a whole damn cask of wine wouldn't work."

Sighing, Maria accepted defeat. "All right. When I spoke with Eden earlier, she said the paperhangers had only worked a few hours and were gone for the day. She and Adams have an appointment with their obstetrician, and Cullen is managing the inn. That means we needn't worry about interruption. So we'll talk now.

"But first, I saw a full pot of coffee in the kitchen. It's probably a little strong and bitter, but maybe you'd like some?"

"To hell with the coffee." Jericho's retort was uncommonly abrupt as he stepped away. "Let's get on with it."

Maria's eyes widened at the anger she saw in his face and heard in his tone. She expected he would be unhappy with her plan, and even try to dissuade her. But she hadn't anticipated this anger bordering on rage. Certainly not before she'd even begun to explain a plan that was sure to disturb him, but not quite so bitterly.

"Wait," she said as much to herself as to Jericho. "We're obviously on different wavelengths. I don't think you understand."

"What's to understand, Maria Elena?"

For the first time since she'd returned to Belle Terre, her name didn't sound like a caress on his tongue. With the intimate camaraderie well and truly destroyed, they faced each other. Two sudden combatants, one angry, one puzzled, locked in a struggle neither expected.

Jericho stood tall and darkly handsome beneath the foyer chandelier, the heat of his anger caught in the play of lights reflecting in hundreds of crystal baubles. Of his mixed ancestry of Scots, French, and American Indian, it was the Indian

blood most apparent in his forbidding features and his coloring.

Only his seething gray gaze proclaimed a lineage of fiery
Scots and passionate Frenchmen.

Maria had never seen him like this. She wondered if anyone
had. "Jericho." With her fingertips she stroked his cheek, then
flushed when he recoiled from her touch. Reining in the flash
of answering anger, she whirled about and stalked away. In
the adjoining drawing room she crossed to a bank of windows
overlooking the scraggly remnants of a long neglected garden.

She thought he would leave. Instead, as she stared through
unseeing eyes at wretched, shriveled shrubs, she heard the
tread of his footsteps on the hardwood floor. As he came to
stand behind her, an uninitiated touch away, a strained silence
stretched like a chasm between them. Maria was first to speak.

"I don't understand." She lifted her gaze to an ancient oak
with massive limbs spreading over most of the lifeless garden.
"Why are you so angry when you don't know what I meant
to say?"

"I know." Jericho's voice was guttural, so soft she barely
heard. "I've known since we woke this morning. I saw it in
your eyes, and heard it in your voice."

"You know?" Maria turned to him then, more puzzled than
before. "You couldn't." Pausing, she looked away in dismay.
This conversation was ridiculous. They were speaking in rid-
dles, avoiding a truth neither understood.

Refusing to be daunted by confusion, Maria faced the man
who was the love of her life. With every ounce of pride, she
challenged her only lover and the seething turmoil that had
chased the love from his eyes. "What is it you think you
know, Jericho?"

"It isn't a matter of thinking, Maria Elena. After two days
of wallowing in a fool's paradise, today the signs were all
there."

"You aren't making sense." In exasperation she gestured
futilely. "What signs, for heaven's sake?"

His face was wooden, beneath the smoldering fire of his gaze. "When you acted so strangely this morning, I knew you were searching for a way to say you were leaving," Jericho continued as if she hadn't spoken. "This time I knew it would be forever. It didn't matter that I understood it was for the best, the very thought made me..." a hand raked cruelly through his hair. "Ah, hell, Maria Elena. You've seen it before, you're seeing now what the thought of losing you does to me."

"Leaving?" Maria's brow wrinkled in denial. "I'm not leaving, Jericho. I never imagined you would think I might. At least not without a fight."

"Who would we fight? Tell me." His arms were tense, the muscles taut, his fists clenched. "How do you do battle with some faceless creature who lives in fear you might recognize and remember him? Or do we fight Belle Terre itself?"

"Both, Jericho." At last she could make sense of his mood. "I fight both, if I must."

I, not *we.* The subtle difference didn't escape a man as astute as Jericho. "Why would you try?"

"Because this is where you belong. Belle Terre is your home, Jericho. One I would share with you. But this time as an equal." The declaration reverberated through the cavernous room. The echo creating a false sense of déjà vu. Though they hadn't had this conversation eighteen years ago, Maria knew now that if she'd asked him to leave Belle Terre with her, he would have.

Nevertheless, if, in the end she must leave again, she still wouldn't ask.

He was far from an unfettered teen now. As the only surviving male of the Rivers family, Jericho was anchored in Belle Terre. Anchored by the responsibility of his widowed and aging *grandmère,* by the needs of his widowed and arthritic mother. Maria would not put him in the impossible position of choosing.

So she would wage the battle for survival and for acceptance on her own terms.

"If you aren't leaving, why this?" Jericho wanted to be done with worrying, and with his abominable mood, but there were questions to be asked, answers he needed. "Why were you pushing me away?"

"Because I needed to think clearly, and I can't when you're near. But if you won't touch me, maybe I can get through this."

Suddenly, she looked so small and vulnerable, he didn't care about questions or answers. He simply wanted to hold her. But, this once, he would respect her wishes. "What is this important thing you must think on?"

Her chin tilted, her shoulder straightened. The woman who met his gaze steadily was an intriguing, heart-stopping coalescence of a concerned and passionate lover with the unique strength of one of Simon's chosen.

Maria was quiet and so lost in composing her thoughts, Jericho began to think she wouldn't respond. Yet when she did, it wasn't the answer he would have wanted.

"I love you, Jericho," she admitted levelly, in a voice that was both strong and tender. "Because I do, and even more because I know you love me, I've been searching for a way to make you understand that this is a battle I must fight alone."

"No!"

Before he could argue more, breaking her own rule, Maria stepped to him, wrapping her arms around his neck. Drawing him down to her, she brushed his lips with hers, teasing the moist, tender flesh until his taut body relaxed. Until his hands burrowed into the spill of her hair deepening the kiss. As if he hadn't just spent two days making love with her until they were both exhausted, he feasted on the sweetness of her kiss like a starving man.

When he lifted his mouth from hers, she rose on tiptoe to steal one last kiss and to whisper against his lips, "Yes."

"Never."

His look was so fierce, so determined, Maria realized she had more than the battle with an unseen assailant and a city on her hands. Her heart ached for this strong, brave man, for the depths of anguish only the strong and the brave suffer for being powerless in a situation that seemed without resolution.

"We can't go on like this, Jericho. It destroys you when you think of what might happen if I stay in Belle Terre. Yet you grow angry at the vaguest suspicion that I might leave. At the same time, a part of me says I'm courting danger by staying. Another whispers I'll lose something that has become as valuable as my life if I go.

"We're both torn in opposing directions time and again, and it has to stop." Her gray gaze held the piercing stare of his. "We have to resolve this."

"And you think you may know how. This is what you needed to think about, my love?" He phrased it as a question, but neither considered it as one. "Why you needed a clear mind."

"Yes." She curled her fingers into her palms to keep from brushing the worry from his face. She mustn't touch him again. Not now. Not yet. "Will you at least keep an open mind? Will you listen to what I have to say before you go totally obstinate on me?"

Obstinate was hardly the proper description. Even so, Maria knew she was seeing only a bit of the steely, unrelenting determination that made Jericho Rivers an exceptional scholar, a star athlete, and a superb lawman. She could easily imagine this was how the half wild Scots must have looked as they ranged the moors for centuries, willing to die defending what was theirs.

Willing to die defending what was theirs. The words struck a chilling chord, and she knew more than ever she had to succeed. "Will you listen, Jericho?" she whispered. "Please."

He wanted to tell her no. He didn't want her to have to fight for anything. What he wanted was to lock her away from every danger, to keep her safe from every hurt. But he knew beyond question that Maria wouldn't hide any more than she would run again. Gradually, a part of his anger abated, but none of his concern. "I'll listen, Maria Elena. Only listen, with no promises."

"No promises," Maria agreed. "From either of us."

When Jericho nodded, his heated gaze strafing over her, she began. "When I was with Josef, I saw the cruelties and savagery of the extremes of prejudice and bigotry. Though I wouldn't compare my experience with the anguish I saw, both spring from the same roots. It was then I realized I have two enemies in Belle Terre.

"One I know. One I don't." She did no more than pause at his look of quickened disquiet. "My first and oldest enemy I must win over. I think I can, by proving my worth, by making it evident I have value that transcends social position or revered family name."

"Belle Terre," Jericho interpreted quietly. "Enemy mine."

"Yes."

"I think the museum gala proved that battle a moot point, Maria Elena. There wasn't a man there who wouldn't have given his soul for a word or a smile from you. Once they got past certain twinges of jealously, so would the women."

"Celebrity." Maria dismissed the fawning of Belle Terre's most notable citizens. "I want enduring respect, but for the ordinary woman, not for any transient fame I might have acquired."

Because he knew she wouldn't listen, Jericho didn't try to tell her there was nothing ordinary about Maria Elena Delacroix Rivers in either of her personas. "How do you plan to win over the unwieldy foe of Belle Terre society?"

"Some of us are born with respect as our birthright. As you were, Jericho. Others aren't so fortunate. But, in the end, we all must be deserving. You, to keep that birthright. While I must prove myself deserving of respect to earn it in the first place.

"That, my darling—" she laughed in wry humor "—is double talk, saying that what you began with, you must work to keep. What I never had, I must work to gain."

"More lessons from Josef's band?" Not double-talk, another glimpse of the wisdom he'd witnessed in the late night interview with Simon McKinzie. But he wouldn't admit it. Not before he heard all she planned. "Is this what your time in the desert taught you?"

Maria's expression of denial was more easily perceived than seen. "It would be more correct to say the desert opened my eyes, and then my mind, making me more willing to accept a lesson from my heart. A lesson on how to have the life and the family I want, here in Belle Terre, with you."

"How will you accomplish this feat?" Jericho was filled with a mix of fear and pride. He wanted to hold her and make the world go away for a while. But he knew it could only be for a little time, so instead, he would wait, he would question, he would listen. "Will Max's millions help you?"

"No. I must earn my place in Belle Terre, not buy it. If I'm accepted as I hope to be, it won't be for money. I will put Max's money to work as he would want it to be used, and soon. But in his name, never mine."

Jericho left her side to cross to a second window overlooking the river. The day was passing rapidly—he would need to go before long. But first, there was another battle plan to discuss. Turning his back to the window, he studied this wise, slender woman, his wife, the mother of his lost child. She was only thirty-five—it wasn't too late for the family they both wanted.

"And your second enemy, Maria?" The quiet question resounded in the vast, empty room. "How will you do battle with a figment, waiting and cowering in the shadows of your mind?"

"I'm going to draw him out of hiding, Jericho," Maria said, as if it were the most simple and easy plan in the world.

Jericho's heart seemed to plummet to his stomach. His

mouth went dry. His teeth clamped over his lip, nearly drawing blood as he caught back an objection. No matter how frightening her plan, he would hear her out. "How will you do this?"

"First, I'll need a list of all our classmates, and anyone else near our age who still lives in the vicinity. If there isn't one readily available, I'll make my own. If I'm going to be visible at all of Belle Terre's social functions, you can be doubly sure I'll be even more visible to each of them."

"Which won't matter to any but the guilty scumbag. He'll think you're stalking him. Perhaps chasing an elusive memory. At first he might even think seeing you on his turf is coincidence. But eventually, on a chance that you might truly remember, he'll come after you."

"Maybe." She didn't add that she was counting on it.

"He has before, Maria Elena. He will again. This time in person, to make sure you truly won't ever remember."

"When he comes, this will be over, Jericho. Then we'll have nothing to fear."

"Nothing to fear?" There was a wildness in his face, as he advanced toward her. A look that said he might catch her up and run away with her. Away from Belle Terre, and the threat that lived within its boundaries. Stopping short, he glared down at her. "This is ridiculous. We can't watch you every minute. We haven't the manpower. Even with Cullen's help, we can't."

"I don't want anyone to watch over me. I can't take the chance he might be scared away." Before he could protest again, she rested her palm against his chest. With the wild beat of his heart rushing beneath her touch, eyes more silver than gray held his steadfastly, as with her own unwavering confidence she sought to calm him. "When we meet, this time it will be on my terms. He won't hurt me, Jericho. I promise."

"How can you be so certain?" The anger was back in Jericho's voice. The anger of fear and tension. "You don't know this man, or what he's capable of doing."

"You're right, I don't know him. But what I do know is better." The hand that lay over his heart curled into a fist, but she didn't take it away. "I know myself. I know what I can do."

Jericho stood rigidly erect, neither moving from her touch nor responding in kind. "You're that sure you can best him?"

"Yes." One gray gaze still held the other. Neither blinked.

"Because of Simon's training."

"After the three weeks of that first, hurried preparation Simon insisted on, there was more. Every few months over the past three years, like all his agents, I've been subjected to rigorous training. Some of it meant to make or break us. In keeping with Simon's theory, better at home than in the field.

"Granted, I would have been no match for an unexpected bomb. In the unlikely chance he, whoever he is, would try that again, I won't be taken unaware. But I don't think he'll go that route a second time any more than you or Yancey do. As you've guessed and I've admitted, thanks to the training Simon requires, in face-to-face, hand-to-hand battles, I can defend myself. Better than the average citizen. Perhaps better than the average policeman."

"No!" Jericho's protest could no longer be held back. "I won't let you do this. It's too dangerous."

"You can't stop me, Jericho. I love you. I don't want to bring you any more grief, but I have to do this—for your sake, for mine, and for our daughter's." Her hand moved from his chest to his arm, catching it, holding him. When he would have drawn away, she kept him, her clasp surprisingly powerful. Surprisingly painful.

"He won once. He lost once. Now he's committed. Short of disappearing completely, do you really think I'll be safe anywhere ever again? This time he has to finish what he's begun. The timing will be his option, the battlefield will be mine."

Releasing his arm, she moved away. "From the moment he put a bomb in my car, I never had any other choice."

Softly, but with unquestionable resolve, she added, "And now, my darling, neither do you."

"Jericho, this won't work." More than a week had passed since their talk at Lady's Hall. Now Maria stood by Eden's sedan, a sheaf of papers in her hand. Jericho waited beside her, towering over her like a great, grim monolith dressed in civilian clothes. "If any one of these people listed here is the right man, he'll be warned off if you're hovering over me like a black cloud."

"If I don't go, Maria Elena, you don't go. If necessary, I'll have you arrested and detained indefinitely." Once it would have been an idle threat, but no more.

"On what charge?" she demanded, trying not to sputter.

"I'll think of something. Count on it." His arms were folded over his chest. The faded plaid of his shirt strained with the pull of tense biceps. Jeans, even more faded, rode low over his hips. The ancient denim molded tautly to his buttocks and thighs as he stood with his booted feet spread and braced, ready for any effort she might make to elude him.

When he'd been convinced she was determined to go through with this, Jericho had declared himself a part of the action. He'd begun by producing a list of suspects his staff had already compiled. A list that had first been cut in two on the basis of gender. Then cut again, systematically, with O'Brian's nosiness and phenomenal memory placing who might have been where and when the night of the bombing.

O'Brian's recollections had been checked, of course. But, almost invariably, they were proven fact, saving an enormous amount of time and effort. Next, five more names had been struck from the list due to debilitating illness or injury.

Because Belle Terre had been a much smaller, much more provincial town eighteen years before, that left seventeen names on the list. But picking a possible assailant out of even that reduced number boggled the mind.

"I'm grateful for your help. I couldn't have gathered the

information so quickly or so thoroughly. But now you've done enough.'' Maria tried a new and desperate tactic, when all others had failed. ''I've already taken up too much of your time. Surely you need to get back to being sheriff again.''

''Nope.''

''Nope?'' She stared up at him, wondering where her chivalrous lover had gone. ''Is that all you have to say?''

''Yep.''

''Good grief! Don't tell me you've been watching old Gary Cooper movies again.'' For a moment Maria was startled that she remembered Jericho's love for Cooper's laconic characters.

''Maybe.'' Jericho shrugged the comment aside.

''Next, I suppose you'll be playing John Wayne. Riding hell-for-leather to the rescue.'' As she uttered the accusation, Maria knew it wasn't true. This was not theatric heroics, he wasn't playing a part. Jericho was simply being Jericho, as he'd always been. First the boy, then the man who would protect her.

Except protection was the last thing she wanted, or needed, if her plan was to succeed.

''Maybe's right.'' Suddenly, her exasperation teetered on the brink of anger. ''Maybe I should sic O'Brian on you.''

As another lift of his shoulders caused his collar to brush the thick thatch of his hair growing low on his neck, he watched her solemnly. Then he smiled for the first time since he'd come to the inn at an early hour that insured he would catch her sleeping. With that success, he'd ordered a breakfast tray for two, asking that it be sent up to the third floor. Then, he'd waited patiently through an ungracious diatribe while she showered and dressed.

The entire time, even over the breakfast she barely nibbled, she'd waged this argument. Carrying it to the elevator, through the halls of the inn, and now the sidewalk, without making a dent in his single-minded purpose. The threat of O'Brian proved how desperate she'd become.

"Call her," Jericho suggested with the mild, unperturbed manner he knew was driving her crazy. Passive resistance, he'd discovered long ago, was safest for a man his size. In any sort of battle, from barroom brawls, to the pursuit of his duty. Now, he found it a handy defense in a lovers' quarrel.

"Be warned," he continued as mildly as before. "Tattling won't do you any good. She'll tell you I'm finally taking advantage of weeks of vacation time accrued over the years."

"Tattling!" Maria began in outrage. Then the rest of what he'd said registered. "Weeks?" She was worried about a day, now he spoke of weeks. "Tell me you didn't say weeks."

"Sorry, love. But, cheer up, it's just four. So far." He tacked on the last as her horror was clearly stamped on her face.

"Jericho." The papers she held crumpled in her hand, but she was too focused on this infuriatingly obstinate man to care. "I have to do this alone. I thought you understood."

"I thought you understood that I have to do it with you." To himself, Jericho admitted that was a lie. A small one, and unrepentant. He expected this reaction and the indignant frustration he saw brewing. But nothing she could say would keep him from spending every second of this dangerous charade with her. From this beginning, to whatever the end might be, he would stay.

"Now, which of us packs a bag?" he asked with what was sure to be infuriating nonchalance.

"Pack a bag." Maria realized she was beginning to sound like an echo. "Why would I pack a bag? Why would you?"

"That depends," he answered cryptically. "Your place or mine, sweetheart?"

When she gave him a look suggesting he was suddenly speaking in tongues, he smiled and explained, "As in where do we sleep?"

"We aren't sleeping...." Biting back her retort, Maria forced a smile in response to the greeting of two elderly strollers. With her lips pursed, she waited until the tittering two tottered beyond hearing. Turning to him, her gray eyes flashing silver fire, she declared through clenched teeth, "Contrary to what you just announced to the biggest gossips of Belle Terre, we aren't sleeping together. I have to do this alone, and I will."

Turning on her heel, she would have stalked away, but Jericho's hands circling her waist swung her back to him. With his fingers splayed over her ribs, their tips touching the undersides of her breasts, he leaned to her. With perfected passive resistance a thing of the past, he spoke in anger. "You shut me out before. For eighteen years you went your own way, did your own thing.

"For half those years I didn't know if you were dead or alive. The other half, I tried to hate you for not coming to me. Dammit, Maria Elena, I'm not a saint and I'm not a martyr. When you waltzed back into Belle Terre like a queen, and twice as lovely, I was angry. To be honest, I wasn't above wanting revenge."

His hands convulsed over her ribs. Tomorrow there would be bruises. Staring at him, seeing, at last, the depths of the pain he'd kept hidden, Maria knew she would never tell him.

"I watched you. I could hardly take my eyes off you all evening. Then I knew the years and the hurt didn't matter. I wanted you, more than I wanted anything." Releasing her, he stepped back. "I won't be shut out, Maria Elena Rivers. Not ever again."

Maria drew a long shuddering breath, understanding him better and loving him more than she thought possible.

"I'll pack a bag." Rising, brushing her lips against his, she whispered softly, "We'll sleep at your house. Together."

Ten

"What on earth?" There was surprise in the halting voice that interrupted a companionable silence. "This is... interesting."

Maria sat cross-legged before the hearth with the mail she'd collected from the inn spread over her lap and spilling on the floor. As she read the card in her hand, her hair fell like a veil against her cheek. Errant ebony strands drifted in a heated draft, mirroring the flickering light of flames in black fire.

Looking up from an urgent report O'Brian had faxed to his study, Jericho allowed himself a moment to appreciate how natural she looked in his home, how right. As always when he caught her in a pensive moment, he wanted to touch her, to feel her passionate response to him. Instead, repressing the stirrings of desire, he asked, "What have you discovered that's so interesting?"

"This." She waggled a stylish and obviously formal card before the light of the fire. "An invitation to attend a private gathering for First Night."

"Oh? What's so interesting about that?"

"Jericho, you know as well as I, First Night is the symphony's premiere concert for the Christmas holiday season. You know better than I that it's restricted to patrons only."

"Patrons and their invited guests," he corrected. "All of whom use the occasion to sit in their seats or private boxes, preening, partying, and gossiping about the rest of the world. Most are more interested in seeing and being seen than in the music."

Biting back his cynical judgment, Jericho damned himself for an insensitive fool when her look of awe faded. "But, all things considered, First Night is always a magnificent performance, and a wonderful evening. So?" A brow arched in question. "Who sent the card? Who invited you?"

Sweeping her hair from her face and holding it, she regarded him steadily. "You?"

"I wouldn't need to invite you, sweetheart. As my date, you won't need an invitation. This is the formality of requesting your presence in a particular opera box."

"Who in Belle Terre would do that?" As she took her hand from her hair, it fell again like a gleaming, midnight mist. Scrambling among the clutter of discarded mail, with no idea how enchanting she was, Maria searched for the matching envelope. When she found it, she went perfectly still.

"Something wrong, love?" Jericho asked with a faint frown creasing his face. The fear of hate mail was never far from his mind. But whatever messages her nemesis might want to deliver, it wouldn't be written on an envelope.

Maria read the return address again, then laid the creamy square in her lap. Lifting her gaze to Jericho's, she murmured, "It's from Letitia Rivers, your grandmother."

Jericho chuckled, inordinately pleased. "Good for her."

Maria's wonder crumpled into disappointed suspicion. "Did you do this? Did you make her invite me?"

"*Make* her?" He made a derisive sound which, in bald terms, would've been called a snort. "When you know her better, you'll understand that no one makes Letitia Rivers do anything.''

"Then did you *ask* her to do it?''

Jericho's dark head turned in denial. "I wouldn't dare suggest it. Not for anyone. Not even for you, my love.''

"Then why would she do this?'' Maria took up the card, reading it again as if she couldn't quite believe it.

"Is there some rule that says the old gal can't recognize quality and a class act all rolled into one? Can it not be that she simply wants your company for the concert?''

Maria dropped the card as if it were hot. "I can't go. I wouldn't know how to act, or what to say. I didn't come prepared, I...'' She stuttered to a stop, at last, drawing a plaintive breath. "I don't have anything to wear.''

Jericho would have laughed at the last, if she hadn't been so deadly earnest. He was convinced Maria would look better than anyone at the concert in anything she chose to wear. Leaving his chair, he went to her, kneeling by her side. Stroking back her hair for the pure pleasure of watching it drift back to her face and throat, because he knew how much it meant to Maria, he made his argument gently. "Of course you can go. If you want a new gown, we can buy one. If not in Belle Terre, then Savannah, or Charleston, or New York, if you like.

"As far as what to say, and how to act? Sweetheart, just be yourself and *Grandmère* will love you.''

"No, I can't.'' Maria shook her head emphatically. "I wouldn't dare.''

Catching her chin between his fingers, Jericho tilted her face to his. "Tell me, since when wouldn't Maria Elena Delacroix Rivers not dare anything?''

"Since now.'' Maria pulled away from his unsettling touch. "Since it's Letitia Rivers who invited me.''

"The grand dame of Belle Terre society. Or better yet, the dragon lady of Belle Terre society. That's her title in private circles. And I know that's exactly what she can be, when the mood strikes." Laughing again, indulgently, Jericho sat beside her. "I should know, I've lived with that imperious burden all my life."

"Burden, my foot." An unsteady, unpolished nail traced the name engraved on the envelope all over again, as if she would stamp it in her memory. "You love her."

"With all my heart." Now, more than ever, Jericho thought, for this unexpected kindness that was more than kindness. Maria had just been given Letitia Rivers's mark of approval. Few in Belle Terre would dare go against the proud and proper octogenarian, if she chose to be Maria's mentor.

"But hasn't she already?" Jericho murmured, remembering when he was thirteen and confused by attitudes. It was his beloved *grandmère* who encouraged him to be Maria's friend.

"What?"

Maria's question drew him from his revere. "Nothing, love." Leaning to her, he kissed the top of her head, letting the clean scent of her hair surround him. "Just remembering."

"Something about your grandmother?"

"Mmm-hmm." Gathering her in his arms, he stared into the fire. "Letitia Rivers is the wisest person I've ever known. With Leah Rivers running a close second, of course."

"Of course," Maria agreed as she snuggled against him. Danger, prejudice, and scandalous heritages were forgotten. Her world, at this moment, was Jericho.

"You're going to like her, and Mother," he predicted.

"The question is, will they like me?" Maria had begun to relax, now she tensed in worry.

"That's already been decided. If it weren't, you wouldn't have the invitation. It's an unwritten rule, scrupulously observed between them, that Letitia does the inviting, with Leah having the right to blackball any of her choices."

"How could they know they like me? Maybe it's not that at all. Maybe they just want a look at the woman their son and grandson is sleeping with."

Straightening and moving from her, Jericho turned her to

face him. "First of all, whom I do, or do not, sleep with is my business and none of theirs. That little bit of family concern was settled long ago. Second of all, if getting a look at you was their only motivation, you would have been invited to a private meeting.

"This, my love, is their stamp of approval. As well as *Grandmère*'s elegant way of flagging her nose at some of the pompous asses whose family closets are filled with more scandalous skeletons than yours could ever be."

Maria's gray gaze moved over his face, seeking a lie of kindness. She saw only honesty. "A stamp of approval for a stranger neither of them knows?" she muttered, "It makes no sense."

"You aren't a stranger. At least not to *Grandmère*. And, if not to her, it's a good bet not to Mother, either."

The fire crackled at Maria's back. Flames leaped and danced, easing the slight chill of the early Low Country winter. In this peaceful place, it would be so easy to believe. She wanted to believe, but the gremlin of reality that whispered in her ear, wouldn't accept blind faith. "How could I not be? How do you know?"

Jericho's hands drifted down her arms, and back again to her shoulders, then her nape. His fingertips stroked the soft skin of her throat. "When we were kids, I had a talk with *Grandmère*."

"About me?"

He only nodded. "She knew quite a lot about you even then. I remember asking her if I should be your friend. Her answer was, yes. To which I replied that was my intention anyway, no matter what she'd said." A low sound rumbled in his chest. One of pride. "Which she never doubted, and wouldn't have had any other way."

"Lady Mary," Maria exclaimed. "She must have spoken with them about me. Perhaps the day we met at her house."

The bell at the front door chimed. Jericho was instantly alert. He'd been so absorbed in Maria, he hadn't heard a car in the drive. Not a good thing, even though anyone bent on harm or mischief would hardly announce themselves with the doorbell. Still, it was a measure of a distraction that couldn't be tolerated.

Excusing himself, he left her among her scattered mail. Court Hamilton waited on the doorstep, still in uniform but obviously off duty. In his arms he held a long, beribboned package.

Jericho's gaze strayed to the pretty parcel. He hadn't ordered anything, nor was he expecting anything. But it was hardly likely Court would be standing on his front steps with a package if it weren't meant for him. Or, the thought struck him, for Maria. "Court! Don't tell me you're subbing for delivery boys now?"

"Miss Leah asked me to deliver this on my way home." Court offered the package, waiting for Jericho to take it.

"On your way home!" As he took the box, Jericho realized it was startlingly light for its size. "Has it escaped my mother's attention that you live quite a distance from here?"

"Actually, sir, I volunteered," Court admitted. "I ran into her at the grocer's. She was buying ingredients for sugar cookies. We just happened to get to talking, and the subject of the package just happened to come up."

"She bribed you," Jericho interpreted. "With the promise of a batch of sugar cookies. A double batch, maybe?"

"Well…" Court grinned then. "Yes, sir, she did. But I consider I got the best end of the bargain."

Of course he thought so. Half Jericho's staff would do anything short of murder or mayhem for his mother, or grandmother—without the bribe of cookies. But when cookies entered the picture, he wasn't so sure about mayhem.

"Would you like to come in for a while, Court? There's coffee in the kitchen. Sorry, no sugar cookies."

"No, sir." Court stepped back, touching the brim of his hat. "I need to get along home. Enjoy your vacation, sir."

Before Jericho could respond, the fledgling officer was hurrying down the walk to his patrol car. Wondering if the younger man had a date, and hoping he did, Jericho closed the door. A pleased look crossed his face as he read the card on the package.

"Something important?" Maria asked, looking up from a stack of letters as he returned. Glimpsing the package adorned by a silver bow, her smile faltered. "Is this a special occasion? Have I forgotten something?" On a teasing note, she asked, "Or should I be suspicious? Is there a secret admirer hiding in your past?"

"The secret admirer is yours, love. So is the package."

When he offered the prettily wrapped box, she didn't touch it. Instead she sat with her hands gripped in her lap. "From you?"

At that moment, Jericho wished he had a gift for her, that he'd put the look of pleasure in her eyes. But, if he were honest and unselfish, he knew a gift from his mother was better. "Sweetheart, I'm definitely an admirer, but the gift isn't from me."

"Then who?" She still hadn't touched the parcel.

"Why don't you see for yourself?" He laid the box in her lap, realizing only then that the sparkling silver bow matched the sparkle in her silver eyes. "Go on," he urged. "Open it."

Like a child who hadn't expected anything for Christmas, then found one present under the tree, she opened it carefully. The bow was removed and the paper neatly folded before she lifted the lid. There, among folds of tissue paper, lay a gown of exquisite lace and shimmering velvet in silver and turquoise.

"It's beautiful," she whispered, barely touching the gown.

Jericho remembered the gown. His father had bought it in Paris and his mother had promptly declared it too wonderful to wear for ordinary occasions. But she'd waited too long for that very special circumstance. Within six months his father had died in a boating accident. Years later, even after shock and grief dulled, because Jared Rivers couldn't see her or dance with her in this wonderful gown of silver and turquoise, she hadn't the heart to wear it.

Instead, she'd packed it away, carefully sealed to preserve it. Now, it seemed, that special occasion had finally arrived. The exquisite creation, a gift of love, had a second chance.

He watched as Maria took the garment from folds of matching silver and turquoise tissue paper with bewildered care. Silver lace gleamed like moonlight on the sea. Turquoise velvet like the sky of a new morning. The classic style was simple, one that would never be outdated. The delicate, yet heavy lace lying over shimmering velvet would flow and cling. Beguiling, teasing, yet oh so proper.

Jericho knew beyond a doubt that before the concert and the festivities of First Night ended, she would drive him mad.

A card caught in velvet and lace fluttered to the floor. The handwritten message and the strong, bold signature were illuminated by dancing flames. As if she couldn't trust her own eyes, Maria whispered, "Read for me, Jericho."

Sitting by her, catching up the card, he read, "'A special gown, for a special occasion that never came, until now. Wear it in happiness, my dear.'" Closing his hand over the card, he looked into eyes bright with unshed tears. "It's signed 'Leah Rivers.'"

"What does it mean?" Maria asked softly. "First the invitation to First Night. Now the gown."

"It means that the two women who have always been a part of my life have chosen to welcome you into the family. Each in her own inimitable style." Drawing the back of his hand over her cheek, with a knuckle he caught the single tear that spilled from her lashes.

A look of alarm leaped into her face. "They don't know…?"

"All they know is that you're here, and that I love you. What they suspect, or even know in their hearts, is another matter," he answered, only a heartbeat before he took her in his arms.

* * *

The morning was unseasonably warm. As the whole week had been, enticing clerks and secretaries and executives alike to spend workday lunch breaks in the bayside park. Maria had come early this Saturday morning, hoping the weekend would offer the opportunity to observe even more of her academy classmates.

As he'd threatened and promised, Jericho strolled with her through the sculpture garden. For the entire week, he'd never been more than a touch away. His study of each man whose name was on her list and who visited the park was as keen as Maria's.

Shirtsleeve weather, as Letitia Rivers called it, had lured the citizens of Belle Terre to the park in droves. Most were there simply to enjoy the pleasant weather. Maria was there to see and be seen. To taunt. To worry. To tempt.

Jericho was hardly her target, but he worried. Worry kept him awake nights long after she slept. Worry usurped his appetite and disrupted his train of thought. None mattered but the last. He didn't need to eat, and he didn't want to sleep while she was at risk. But he, by damn, needed to think clearly and rationally in order to protect her.

Though she hid it most times, and even put it aside at others, Maria resented his intrusion. In her mind, this was her battle— to fight alone. But Jericho would have none of it. Thus far, he'd won that particular battle, but the day was coming...

Breaking off a thought he wasn't ready to face, he walked beside her, watching, as she did, with believable nonchalance. No one but Jericho knew that his casual posture was a total lie. Or that his thumb was tucked at his waist to afford a smooth, easy reach for the small handgun holstered beneath the loose denim shirt he wore over a formfitting, unhampering T-shirt.

No, he didn't expect trouble in the park. But he hadn't expected a bomb, either. So he would be watchful, this time, for what he didn't expect.

"Over there." He interrupted their silent stroll, waiting until she looked in the direction he indicated. "Johnny Cavender, there by the fountain. He brought his son today."

Maria had seen Cavender before. The slender man was one of the few who brought a bag lunch to the park each day. If he recognized Maria, or was uncomfortable at all, it never showed.

"The boy looks happy." The boy was small, but Maria knew he was nine. Maria knew a great deal about the boy, and his father. "He seems to have adjusted to his mother's illness."

Jericho watched the child toss a horseshoe, then listened to the clang of the post as it hit home. "It took some time, mental illness is tough for a kid to understand. Johnny's good with him, and his wife's mother helps, but mostly they're a father-son team.

"Does seeing Johnny out of his three-piece suit and in jeans trigger a memory, or an idea?" Jericho had studied Maria's reaction throughout the morning. Hoping there would be some remembrance, however small. Something he could act on, ending this quest, taking her out of danger.

"Nothing." She didn't look away from the man and his son as the sound of a gleeful giggle drifted to them. "But I think it would be safe to say Johnny's name can be stricken from the list. In fact, I think everyone we've seen this week can be dismissed as suspects."

"Why?" Jericho had arrived at the same conclusion. But he wanted to hear her reasons for the decision.

"They all seem too normal. Too comfortable with my presence here. No one evaded me, or stopped coming to the park because I was here." Completing her reasons, she added, "Not one avoided looking me in the eye."

"So you think everyone here is innocent."

"Yes."

"Or one is a damned good actor."

Maria sighed sadly. "If I'm wrong, he's too good."

That was scary, but Jericho knew there was no help for it. Drawing her down to a bench beyond the splash of an ornate fountain, Jericho took her hand. "We've caused quite a stir ourselves."

"Because all of Belle Terre thinks I'm your mistress?" Maria could easily imagine the gossips whispering that blood would always tell, and Maria Elena Delacroix was running true to historic, wanton, and shocking Delacroix form.

"There may be suspicions that we're sleeping together, but only a trusted few know for sure." With his fingers laced through hers, he stroked her palm, and felt her shiver. Grinning wickedly, pleased with this minute diversion, intent on capitalizing on it, he murmured, "But I'm sure titillated imaginations are running amok."

"It didn't help my reputation that you kissed me under the rose arbor, in sight of anyone who cared to look."

"Say the word and I'll make an honest woman of you."

"That's what this is all about, isn't it?" Maria flexed her fingers over his but didn't pull away. "You're making sure everyone thinks I belong to you. You're warning *him* away with it."

Jericho couldn't deny the accusation. She was right, he was hoping their obvious connection would avert danger. He wanted to catch the bomber in the worst way. But not with Maria as bait.

Though she wanted and expected an answer, he tossed her his most engaging smile and evaded. "Sweetheart, anyone who's ever known you understands that no one owns you."

Owning and belonging weren't quite the same in this case, but Maria knew evasion even when he dressed it up in a provocative smile. Rather than quarrel over something she couldn't change, Maria changed the subject instead. "I've seen a young boy in a wheelchair here everyday. He was feeding the squirrels by the water fountain when we arrived. He's too young to be alone, yet there never seems to be anyone with him."

"That's Joey Sims. His dad works here in the park. Tom can't afford day care, so he brings the boy with him every day. On pretty days, he lets him roam the park. Though Tom makes it a point to be nearby, because everyone loves Joey, they look after him."

"When it isn't good weather? What happens then?"

"Tom drives and does some gardening for my mother and grandmother. When it rains, and he can't work in the park, one or both find something for him to do around the house. They each like for Joey to visit, and they've been known to argue over him."

"What happened? What put Joey in the chair?"

"An auto accident. Tom's wife was driving. She hit a bridge abutment on a deserted road and walked away with only a scratch. Joey wasn't as fortunate. He suffered a head injury, and his spine was broken. That was three years ago, on his second birthday."

Maria's lips pursed in a question. "You said his mother escaped the wreck virtually unharmed. Where is she now?"

Jericho muttered an uncomplimentary name in utter disgust. "Who knows? When I said she walked away, I mean literally. She left Joey in the car, walked to the main road, hitched a ride with a trucker, then disappeared.

"At the time of the accident, Tom was working seven-to-seven on the second shift at a plant. The next morning he reported them missing. Because the road was one she wouldn't normally travel, we were a half day finding the car. Two more days were spent searching for Ellie, hoping she hadn't wandered off into the swamp. Thinking she might've been disoriented, we checked the main road and the truck stops. That's when we found the trucker who gave her a lift.

"He gave a written statement saying that when she flagged him down, she was bleeding but not badly injured and, in his words, 'drunk as a skunk.'"

Maria's heart ached for the frightened, injured baby crying for his mother most of a night and part of a day. She could only imagine the father's anguish. "Tom Sims must be a good man."

"He is. Maybe a little too proud."

"A Sims family moved onto my street shortly before I left Belle Terre. But there were two boys."

"It's the same family. Tom's parents still live on your old street. Tony, his older brother, was killed in a tank in Desert Storm. Tom's a real hard-luck case. Along with everything else, his father is senile and his mother's heart is failing."

"But he works every day?"

"Every day, except when Joey's sick."

"Poor man. Can no one help him?"

"We've tried, Maria Elena. His damnable pride won't let him accept charity, even for Joey. If he was starving, maybe. But it would have to be that drastic."

Rising from the bench, her fingers drawing slowly from Jericho's, Maria turned in a circle. For as far as she could see, the park was immaculate. Not one weed grew among the shrubs. No scraps of paper dotted the walks. Every bench looked as if it had been freshly painted. "He does this alone?"

"Joey's medical bills were horrendous. They still are." Jericho knew he needn't elaborate. One look at Joey told that tale. "Tom could make more in the factory, but then he couldn't spend time with Joey. To make sure this job wouldn't be charity, and to do it right, he studies gardening and park management by correspondence. He's been known to work twenty-hour days, sleeping just four hours a night. But it means they're together, and Joey's not cooped up inside some institution."

"How often is he too tired to do anything but fall asleep at night? How often is Joey alone then?"

"Only Tom and Joey know that, sweetheart."

"And he absolutely won't accept any help?" Maria's face was marked with concern as she searched for the boy.

"None." Following the direction of her gaze, Jericho realized Joey sat by the fountain, watching two children play in the nearby wading pool. "Sometimes I wonder if Tom feels he must do it this way as penance for letting Joey get hurt."

Maria understood the need for penance. She knew the black abyss of grief and guilt that always waited. She knew second guessing, and the long, angry hours spent wondering Why didn't I...? or Could I have...? There were countless questions Tom Sims would ask himself over and over. But the worst was, What if...? And the shattered hopes and dreams it recalled.

It was, in part, penance that had driven her from Belle Terre and Jericho. Penance that made her believe she was undeserving of help. But Maxie hadn't listened.

Neither would she.

"What if there was a way?" Returning to the bench, Maria slipped her hand into Jericho's again. "How would he refuse financial help if the donor was anonymous? He couldn't give it back if he didn't know where or how."

"What are you thinking?" With his free hand Jericho brushed her hair from her cheek, letting his fingertips linger at the pulse at her throat. "What's going on in that enterprising mind of yours?"

"Last time it was steel trap," Maria commented absently, her attention, for once, divided between Jericho and the surrounding scene.

"Same thing." He laughed, pleased by this distraction. "So, let's hear it. What are you planning for Joey and Tom?"

"I'm not sure yet."

"But you're thinking this sort of quiet benevolence would please Maxie."

Maria's preoccupied look cleared as she smiled back at him. She liked that he called it "quiet benevolence." A name that described exactly what she wanted. A far better description than charity. Her elderly friend and mentor would approve.

Jericho and Maxie couldn't have been more different, yet they were very much alike in what mattered. Maria wished again the two most important men in her life could have known each other.

"Quiet benevolence," she murmured, certain now of what she wanted to do. "All I have to do now is come up with a plan, and decide exactly how to go about making it reality."

"In the meantime, if you've done enough sleuthing for the day, let's go home." Standing, he tugged her to her feet, drawing her close until her breasts brushed his chest. "I have a plan for the rest of the day, and I know exactly how to make it reality."

"Ah, you do, do you?" Suddenly more lighthearted than she'd been in a long, long while, Maria was giddy with purpose and love. Not caring that the park was filled with strollers and romping children and likely gossips, she locked her fingers at his nape. Drawing him down to her, she whispered against his lips, "You wouldn't want to tell me about it now, would you?"

"I'd rather show you."

"But not here."

"Not a good idea." His lips teased over hers, making promises. "Unless you want to see the sheriff of Belle Terre arrested by one of his own deputies."

"Which would really throw the proverbial monkey wrench into your plans for the rest of the day."

"'fraid so." His hands moved down her back to her waist, then drifted over her ribs, his fingertips skimming wickedly, daringly, over the sides of her breasts.

Stepping from his embrace, Maria caught his hand. "Then we should hurry."

Jericho's answering grin was as wicked and as tantalizing as his touch. "We should, my love. Ah, yes, indeed we should."

Eleven

"**Y**ou look like you needed this an hour ago." As she spoke over the bedlam in the gymnasium, Eden set a cup of tea before Maria.

"Try *two* hours ago." Maria smiled as Eden sat down, her own cup in her hand. "In my estimation the turnout has been terrific."

"In anyone's estimation, the turnout has been *better than* terrific. In fact, in all my time as chairman of the hospital holiday blood drive, we've never been as successful." Turning a radiant but tired look at Maria, Eden added, "Thanks to you."

"I'm pleased that I could help with the publicity."

"The TV campaign with you as our spokesperson helped," Eden agreed. "But your willingness to donate your time to the Red Cross did more. So did the cheesecakes you baked for the goody table."

Maria's expression grew rueful. "I can't take credit for doing more than stirring and mixing. The recipe belonged to an old friend. It was the specialty dessert of his restaurant.''

Eden had grown accustomed to learning of Maria's past tidbit by tidbit. Knowing there would be more gradually, she would wait. ''The best part has been the way you've helped in person. I've heard several of the other volunteers who were your classmates at Belle Terre Academy say that seeing you like this makes you seem less intimidating and more approachable than you were in school.''

''Intimidating?'' Maria turned a startled face to Eden. ''Me?''

''Good grief, yes.'' Eden set her cup aside. ''I was four years behind you, but even those of us in the lower grades stood in awe of your brains and your confidence. And, of course, your looks.''

''You're joking.'' Maria stared at this woman who was the most beautiful person she knew. ''You have to be.''

''I'm not joking,'' Eden assured her. ''You were quiet and so all-together, you didn't seem to need or want anyone close. Except Jericho. And who could stop our gentle giant from going anywhere? Even into unwanted friendships, at the risk of rejection.''

''Unwanted friendships?'' Maria frowned. ''I never... I wouldn't have rejected...'' Suddenly her puzzled gaze narrowed. ''You're telling me this for a reason, aren't you, Eden?''

Taking up her tea, Eden sipped, then returned the cup to the table. With her hands going to the small bulge of her pregnancy, she said thoughtfully, kindly, ''I suppose I am. But I'm not sure you want to hear what I've discovered.''

''Of course I do. I value your friendship and your opinions.'' Maria didn't explain that Eden Cade was her first real female friend. As with all men, except Jericho and Maxie, the women whose paths crossed hers had never been more than acquaintances. Getting to know Eden had been a rare pleasure.

Her friendship, an even rarer treasure. "There isn't anything you can't say to me."

Eden considered Maria's protest for a long moment, then took the risk of speaking her thoughts. "We're a lot alike, you know. If we'd been of an age, I think we both would have seen it years ago. We set ourselves apart. I did, and Adams became my champion. You did, and Jericho was there.

"I won't say our circumstances weren't different, and I won't say old attitudes didn't play a part in your life. But, I know now there were boys and girls who would've reached out to you and to me, if we'd let them. Thank God, Adams and Jericho refused to recognize or be discouraged by the boundaries we erected around us."

"I was given a second chance," she explained. "Now you have one, too. Look around you. There are women and men here who would be your friend. Not because you've come home a celebrity, but for the woman you've shown you are on days like today."

Struggling from her chair, with a palm pressed against the small of her back, Eden grinned ruefully. "In the vernacular of our beloved men, the marker's on the ten-yard line, Maria. It's first and goal, and you have the ball. What happens next is up to you."

As Eden turned away, Maria chuckled at the analogy and searched the dispersing crowd for Jericho. Without intruding on her space, he waited nearby. As he had from the day he rescued her spilled books and walked with her to her first class at the academy. As he had until she left him. And now, again.

Eden made a vivid point. One that hit home. Maria wondered where she would be, what she would be, if Jericho had been frightened away by a misfit's boundaries. She wondered what life with Jericho might have been like if the boundaries hadn't existed.

Rising to return to her assigned tasks, Maria knew Eden's obliquely suggested point was on target. She was well on the way to earning the respect of Belle Terre at large. Now it was time to let down her guard and open the door to friendships.

"Long day, love?" Pausing in conversation to greet her, Jericho draped an arm around Maria's shoulder, drawing her close.

"A good day." Three hours had passed since the talk with Eden. When the throng dwindled to only a few stragglers, Maria moved, with a new perspective, among the volunteer staff, discovering how right Eden had been. The smile she gave Tom Sims was tired but contented. "It's good to see you again, Tom."

"It's good to see you again, too, Miss Delacroix." The man who stood by Jericho blushed from neck to hairline, but his greeting was pleasant. "I've been wanting to thank you for the bird books you gave Joey. Everyone who comes to the park is good to him, but you're the first to take so much interest in what he likes. Except Miss Eden and the two Mrs. Rivers, of course.

"Speaking of Joey, if you'll excuse me, I need to make a quick check on him. Mrs. Cade likely has a chore or two for me, as well." Tom backed away, turned abruptly, and hurried off.

"Goodness," Maria murmured. "I didn't mean to chase him away. Did I interrupt a private conversation?"

"Not so private." Jericho tangled his fingers in her hair as it brushed over her shoulder. "We were playing twenty questions."

"You were questioning Tom about something?"

"Just the reverse. He was questioning me." Jericho's gray gaze followed Tom Sims. "About you."

"About me?" Maria exclaimed worriedly. "You don't think he's suspicious about the grant to the park, do you?"

"Sweetheart." Jericho hugged her close and kissed her forehead. "Why would he be suspicious of fact? In Maxie's name you made a grant to the park. The one stipulation the grant carried was that the person responsible for its excellent care and condition be given a semiannual bonus. It's been done, legally and through proper channels. It can't be called charity because Tom deserves it. So how could he object? Why would he be doubtful?''

When she would have questioned more, unmindful of watchful eyes, he stopped her with a second, glancing kiss. ''Tom's asking about you because he's no different from the rest of the town. You're its hottest topic. Your name is on every tongue.''

''Because of this?'' Diverted and soothed, Maria covered his hand with hers. With her fingertips she stroked the gold band he wore, knowing that someday soon she and Jericho must make some explanations. Once they understood what the explanations were themselves. ''Is there gossip because of us?''

''Of course. Gossip is what small towns do best,'' he admitted. ''But it's more than gossip, and it's mostly about what you're doing. In a short time, you've made your mark on the community. You've brought Belle Terre to its knees, Maria Elena.''

''Except for the diehards and naysayers.''

''The world will always have its share of both. We can't let that ugly, small-minded factor ruin the good things.''

''I won't. Having half of Simon's staff standing watch has made times like this possible. Because of you, and with their help, I've been able to interact with the community, without constantly looking over my shoulder, always wondering.''

Jericho didn't deny the presence of The Black Watch. After Simon's visit, though added protection was never discussed, it was a foregone conclusion. It wasn't the first time the Scot had set a phalanx of agents to watch over another. It wouldn't be the last. As Maria continued her search, becoming more visible in the community, Jericho was grateful for the added manpower, and for the expertise.

''So?'' With a tilt of his head, he looked down at her. ''First there was the toy drive. Which, like the park, reaped the benefits of the mysterious Maxie's quiet benevolence and your hard labor. Then the benefit for the children's wing at the hospital. Now the blood drive. What's next, dear heart?''

''I leave that to Eden. When it comes to community service, she's indefatigable.'' Maria laughed. ''Considering her condition, to save face, the least I can do is keep up with her.''

''Speaking of Eden, it looks like she's asked Tom to close the doors. That means she's calling an end to the drive. I'd say it was a resounding success.'' Jericho smiled down at Maria. ''For the community, and for you.''

''I learned a lot about Belle Terre today, Jericho.'' Maria took his hand as the room began to empty. Thoughtfully, she amended, ''But, thanks to Eden, I learned even more about myself.''

''Do you recognize the car, Court?'' It was ironic that one of the few times circumstances prevented Jericho from accompanying Maria home from another of what was becoming almost daily community projects, there was a strange vehicle sitting in the drive.

''Yes, ma'am. The sedan belongs to the sheriff's mother. Guess this means her arthritis is acting up worse than usual. That would explain why she's not been out and about the past few weeks. If she's taken to the pool, it's bad.'' Stopping the squad car, he crossed to the passenger side, doffing his hat when Maria stood by him on the drive. ''I can go in with you, check things out.''

''No, thank you, Court. Mrs. Rivers and I will be fine.''

''Don't be alarmed if you see someone moving about the place. Usually, when Mrs. Rivers comes out, Tom Sims drives her. He does a little yard work while she's inside.''

''I'll be fine, Court.'' Maria wished assuring the deputy a second time would make it true. ''I know you have more important things to do than play watchdog for me.''

Once the deputy was on his way, Maria hurried inside, wondering what she should do about Leah Rivers. Should she seek the older woman out, introduce herself, and thank her for the extraordinary gift of the gown? Or leave her in peace?

Maria's indecision was resolved when she found Joey in the den, sitting before the TV, watching a Disney movie. With his eyes round and his mind preoccupied by this rare treat, he repeated the message he'd been charged to give to either Sheriff Rivers or Miss Delacroix.

"You're sure she wants company in the solarium?" Maria asked, to be certain the boy wasn't too caught up in the movie to convey the message correctly.

"Yes, ma'am," the five-year-old assured her solemnly. "Miz Rivers had me say it two times."

"Thank you, Joey." Maria brushed the soft blond hair from his face and kissed his cheek and neck until he shivered and giggled. Straightening from him, she asked, "Is there anything I can get you, or anything I can do for you before I go?"

"No, ma'am. Miz Rivers already got me some cookies and juice. If I need anything else, my dad will be watching the window. All I have to do is roll my chair over there, and he'll come running. Also, I got my bird picture book, I can see some of them in the marsh, even from here. Dad can read me their names at home."

"You manage pretty well by yourself, don't you, Joey?"

"I try," the boy answered solemnly, the book clasped tightly in his hands. "So my dad won't have to work so hard."

So my dad won't have to work so hard. His words followed Maria as she went to the bedroom to freshen up. The memory of the frequency and the fondness with which the child spoke of his father went with her to the solarium, as well.

She'd just stepped on the stairway when a voice sounded above the quiet splash of the pool. A voice with clipped tones softened by four decades spent in the South.

"Hello, Maria Elena. And a belated welcome to Belle Terre."

Leah Rivers looked much as Maria remembered. Not very

tall, dark hair going silver in shining streaks. Her body trim, and barely a little heavier than years ago. Only her slightly swollen knees and knuckles marred an amazing youthfulness.

"Come join me." Leaning back on the banquette that circled the pool, Leah gestured in welcome. "Better yet, come have a glass of wine while we get acquainted." Before Maria could respond, she moved deeper into the water and, with practiced strokes, crossed the pool. Surfacing near the bottom stair, she tossed back her streaming hair. "It's past time we met again, don't you think?"

"Yes, I suppose it is." When she took a seat at the table with the wine bucket at its side, Maria knew it was more than past time she met Jericho's mother.

Leah Rivers stepped from the pool, plainly rejuvenated by the churning, heated water. With careful moves, she patted herself dry, slipped into a warm robe, and joined Maria at the table. "So, my dear…" Filling two glasses and taking one for herself, she leaned back in her chair, studying Maria through eyes that were carbon copies of Jericho's. "How are you, really?"

"Really?" Maria pondered the qualification, wondering what to make of it. Leah resolved the question for her.

"Jericho has told us you're coping quite well. But I know having a worried, overprotective man hovering constantly can be exhausting. For the record, I've learned that the best help for it is to remember he loves you, and has loved you most of his life."

Pausing in her monologue, Leah considered Maria's bewildered look. "You didn't realize that I know Jericho loves you?"

Maria only turned her head from side to side, then finally managed to ask, "He told you?"

"Of course not. At least not in words. But I know my son. Given his recent behavior, it would have been a simple deduction, even if I didn't know him so well." In a gesture strongly reminiscent of Simon McKinzie's five fingers folding into a fist as he made his points, Leah began her enumerations. "First of all, you were the only girl in his life. Even in college, he didn't date. Oh, he made a try at it, but nothing worked out. In fact the effort only made him more miserable. Later, in football, then here in Belle Terre, he lived like a monk."

Sipping from her glass again, Leah grinned. "Not from lack of willing partners, though. He's had friends who were ladies, but never a lady friend—if you understand the distinction." Lifting a brow, she waited for Maria's nod of understanding before returning to her monologue. "For eighteen years it was the same story.

"Then you walked back into the picture. Four hours later, he brought you here, to his home. And, I hope, to his bed."

As a blush colored Maria's cheeks and swept to her throat, Leah chuckled. "Forgive me for being so blunt, but it is the only explanation. I'm just sorry this damnable arthritis flared up so badly I couldn't be at the museum to see for myself. Lord knows, I've waited long enough for your return."

"You waited for my return?"

"Of course. Jericho is obviously a one-woman man. And you, my dear, are clearly that woman." Splayed fingers closed into a loose fist, and the older woman reached again for her glass.

"You don't mind?" Maria asked, when she found her voice.

"Mind?" Leah's brows shot up again as she contemplated and interpreted the question. "That you were a Delacroix? Good grief, has that boy not told you about me?"

"That you don't give a damn whose father made what fortune when and how? Or whose grandfather led what charge where and when? Or even whose great-great-granddaddy signed what great document, if any?" Maria's smile bloomed. Next she chuckled. Then she laughed, in part because this small woman called the tall, handsome man who was her only child, a boy. Imagining what life had been like with a mother and grandmother like Leah and Letitia Rivers, Maria murmured, "Oh, yes, Jericho told me."

"Good," Leah said crisply. "Then we understand each other and can be friends. But only so long as you don't hurt him."

"If I do," Maria said calmly now that she had found her footing with this woman, "it will be to prevent a greater hurt."

Leah studied her over the rim of her glass. Silver eyes only a little faded by age probed silver eyes filled with love for her son. At last her chin dipped in assent. "Fair enough."

"Hey, you two," Jericho called from the top step. "Is this a private conversation, or can anyone join in?"

Maria looked at Leah, waited for her subtle agreement, then called, "Of course you can join us. I was just about to thank your mother for the silver gown."

"And I was just about to tell Maria Elena the gown will be a perfect match for her eyes." Leah chuckled under her breath and drained her glass. "So, why don't you come on down and pour your mother another glass of your wine?"

"*My* wine?" Jericho asked over the clatter of his booted heels on the spiral stairs. "And who's driving?"

"Of course it's your wine," Leah drawled as he kissed her cheek, then took a seat between them. "And Tom's driving. As usual."

"So, Mother." Lacing his fingers through Maria's, ignoring Leah's teasing, he asked bluntly, "What do you think of my wife?"

Leah didn't bat an eye, and Maria's suspicion that she'd known all along was confirmed.

"What do I think of her?" Leah reached across the table, covering Maria's free hand with her own. "I think it was love at first sight for your grandmother and me, as well."

"You're not surprised?"

"You're a one-woman man, my dear. Some men meet that one woman, and the love of a lifetime, when they're older and the time is right. You met the love of your life too soon, then had to spend a little while growing up.''

"I've been grown up for a long time, Mother."

"Ah-hh, but the difference is that now the time is right."

"Almost," Maria interjected in a low voice.

"Yes," Leah agreed. "Almost."

An agreement that brought that particular subject to a close, leaving Jericho and Maria wondering what else this astute woman knew of their lives. As she raised her refilled glass in a silent toast to her son and the woman who was his life, Leah Rivers offered no answers.

Papers skidded across the hearth, and landed on smoldering coals. With her arms folded at her waist, Maria watched as one sheet caught fire. Then another. Information meticulously gathered and recorded, then proved useless, scorched and shriveled, then crumbled into flaming ash.

"Useless," Maria muttered. "All of it, utterly useless."

"What are you doing?" Jericho stood in the doorway, returning from a late night of catching up on paperwork. His gaze moved from Maria to the fire and back again, as he recognized the files containing all the information she'd spent week upon week compiling. "Why, Maria?"

"Why not?" she asked bitterly. "There's nothing there. In all this time of digging and delving and watching, what do we have to show for it? Every name on the list is squeaky clean. Or too blasted sharp to leave even a single clue."

"Yancey warned us." Setting down his briefcase, Jericho came to her, taking her in his arms. Holding her, he waited until the tensions eased from her and her taut muscles relaxed. As she leaned back against him, with his lips touching her temple, he murmured, "What now? Where do we go from here?"

Crossing her arms over his, Maria stared into the fire, seeking answers that weren't there. As the day had slid into evening, she'd lit the fire rather than turn on the lights. Now, while its flames flickered in the fall of darkness, she drew a defeated breath. "When I started this, I was so sure I could find him. So sure everything would work out. Now, I don' think so."

"He could be miles away by now," Jericho suggested.

"Or he could be a mile down the road, waiting and worrying that one day I might remember him."

"But you don't, sweetheart."

"And you don't think I ever will."

It was Jericho's turn to watch the flames, then catch a harsh breath. "No, love, I don't think you'll ever remember."

"But he doesn't know. If he did, he wouldn't dare trust that the memory wouldn't surface. I wouldn't want to base my life on that shaky premise, do you?"

Jericho released her and backed away, waiting until she turned to face him. "Whose life are you speaking of? His? yours?"

"I wish it could be that simple. Just him. Just me. But that can't be. My life affects every other life I touch. We've been so sure he's harmless. But is he? In his efforts to frighten me away, he hurt a boy. Next time it could be you, or your mother. Or Eden and her unborn child.

"I can't take that risk." Tears spilled down her cheeks. With the heel of her hand, she scrubbed them away. " couldn't live with the knowledge that I caused any of you harm."

Jericho's arms hung impotently at his sides. He would do battle to keep her. If the enemy had a face. "You've decided you have no recourse but to leave, haven't you?"

Maria spun away, but not before he saw new tears glittering on her cheeks. "He's won the last battle. I won't come back again."

"Because you love me."

"Yes. Nothing will ever change that."

Turning her to him, with a palm at her nape and his thumb at the line of her jaw, he tilted her face to his. "Then, will you give me one last promise? No questions asked, just the promise.''

''I can't.''

''One last promise for what we've lost. For what we'll never have.'' He knew what he asked was unfair. But he was desperate enough to try anything to keep her for even a little while longer. ''Please, love. One promise, no more.''

Maria couldn't refuse, ''All right.''

''Say it.''

''I promise.''

Jericho's mouth swooped down on hers. He wouldn't ask for much, but every extra minute was precious.

When he drew away, with her body aching for his, Maria questioned hoarsely, ''What have I promised?''

''You promised me the holidays.'' Her lips were parting to protest when he kissed her, until both were breathless and desperate, and the bedroom was much too far away. Making quick work of their clothing, on an afghan flung over the floor, he made love to her while the fire blazed, and the remnants of their quest turned to dust.

''We'll find a way,'' Jericho vowed when the storm of need ended. ''Somehow, we will find a way.''

Lying with her cheek pressed against his chest, listening to the quieting thunder of his heart, Maria didn't speak as she stared into the fire and the ashes of lost dreams.

''This is wrong.'' Maria stood before the mirror in Jericho's bedroom. She wore the gown of silver and turquoise. ''I shouldn't be going to the concert. We shouldn't have planned the announcement party at Lady's Hall afterward. Planning anything so public with me could be dangerous.''

''No.'' Jericho finished with his black tie and opened a dresser drawer. Taking out a sleek velvet box, he crossed to her. ''The word that you're leaving after the holidays has been duly circulated. He'll know he's safe now. He'll know he's won.''

"Again," Maria said bitterly. As he stood behind her, their gazes met in the mirror. "If it were just the danger to me, I wouldn't go."

"I know." Catching a lock of black hair falling from a charming, temptingly perfect chignon, Jericho tucked it away.

"I can't risk—"

"Shh." With the stroke of his fingers, he stopped her. "I know, Maria Elena. I truly know. You're a compassionate and generous woman. In two days it will be Christmas, a time of kindness and unexpected miracles. There's no reason we can't hope for one."

"We did everything in our power to make our own miracle, Jericho. Instead we traveled down one blind alley after another." Lifting a shoulder wearily, she whispered, "Perhaps miracles aren't meant for people with unforgiving hearts."

"Perhaps. But there's no rule that forbids wishing."

"What do we wish on, Jericho?" Maria caught a shaking breath. Turquoise shimmered and caressed. Silver sparkled and clung and enticed, but only Jericho noticed. "The first evening star?"

"We could wish on this." Opening the long box, he took out a chain of silver and gold. When he fastened it around her neck, a turquoise heart wrapped in delicate twining filigree lay in the cleft of her breasts. "A captive heart. As my heart was taken captive forever by a young girl."

Maria's eyes sparkled as silver as the lace. As she went into his arms, his name was a caress. "Jericho."

Jericho's *grandmère* was exactly as Maria expected. Bold, brash, caustic, a bit arrogant, and funny. Letitia Rivers was the epitome of irreverence in elegant dress. Her hair was thick, and completely white. But she shared her coloring and features with Jericho. It was as easy to see this unique lady was likely the genetic source of his great size.

"Horsey," she grumbled as Maria sat on one side of her and Leah on the other. "That's what women like me were called in my day. But—" a smile curled her lips and a twinkle lit her eyes as she looked past Maria to her grandson "—it worked well for Jericho, wouldn't you say?"

"I would."

"Speak up girl," the old woman demanded imperiously. "I can't hear you above that infernal racket below us."

The infernal racket below the Rivers's private box was the general audience finding their seats, while the orchestra warmed up. Even with the furor, her voice soared through the auditorium.

"Yes," Maria spoke louder. "It works well for Jericho. And for you, too, Mrs. Rivers."

"My name's Letitia. Mrs. Rivers is too much a mouthful to say at every turn." Lifting a lorgnette, she studied the crowd. "Tell me, Maria Elena, what happened to that handsome scalawag who was your father?"

"He and my mother retired to Florida."

"Retired, did he?" As she looked down, a pudgy man glanced up at the Rivers's box, caught sight of Maria, and turned his back. "From running scams on the streets, maybe. But not drinking, I'll wager."

"No," Maria sighed, as Jericho slid his hand over hers, and Leah shrugged in helpless commiseration. "Not from drinking."

"I didn't think so. And I'd wager, as well, his retirement is on your dime." Expecting no answer, Letitia leaned over the rail, her glare riveted on the haughty, pudgy man, her voice rising a decibel. "You know, Harvey Kendrick, it always puzzled me how a pompous ass who worked his scams in the boardroom and threw his drunks in a mansion could feel superior to the daughter of a man who did the same thing on the street.

"Would you tell me how, Harvey?" Spurred on by Jericho's not-quite-stifled chuckle, Letitia leaned farther over the rail. "I asked you a civil question, Harvey. I expect a civil answer."

The auditorium was quiet, all attention riveted on Letitia and her target. Even the orchestra waited for his answer.

"Oh, Harvey," Letitia's voice was lilting. "Why so silent, when you usually have so very much to say? Cat steal your tongue?"

Harvey Kendrick rose from his seat, stretching to his fullest height. Which, shoulder to shoulder, would have been six inches shorter than Letitia. "Dammit, Letitia, are you drunk?"

"Are you?" she shot back. "It's your usual state, isn't it? It's no wonder poor Lucy died young. You drove your pretty wife to an early grave with your drinking. Along with the whoring, that is."

A titter began in the back of the auditorium, then swelled to guffaws. In the bedlam, Harvey Kendrick chose to run for cover.

When he was gone, Letitia muttered under her breath to Maria, "Thank you, my dear. I've wanted to do that for a long time."

Maria's face was flushed, but Jericho and Leah acted as if this were a common occurrence. "You're welcome, Letitia," she managed as Jericho squeezed her hand. "But what did I do?"

"You gave me a good reason." Leaning back in her chair, the old woman smiled like the proverbial Cheshire cat. "That will teach the arrogant pip-squeak to shun *my* granddaughter-in-law."

"You're repeating yourself, *Grandmère,* but that's telling him." Jericho smothered a grin.

"Thank you, Jericho. I'm glad you liked it, my dear."

The laughter died. The conductor, a young and attractive man, strolled onstage. Bowing left, then right, he paused. Lifting his laughing gaze to the naughty octogenarian, he bowed again. "With your permission, Letitia, we'll begin."

"Then by all means, begin, Daniel."

"Thank you." Turning, his baton raised, with a masterful, slashing stroke of his arm, the hall filled with music.

Twelve

Lady's Hall was Old World refinement and sophisticated simplicity reincarnate. Restored to the grandeur of its past, shimmering in holiday splendor, it seemed suspended in time. A blend of the best of the past with New World comfort.

Tucked in the curve of the foyer stair stood a massive fir, its limbs weighted by ornaments and lights, almost brushing a domed ceiling. Throughout the house, the festive spirit was repeated in garlands of evergreen and flowers bedecking walls and doors. In nooks and corners, massive, antique urns overflowed with more evergreens and berries, with poinsettias and white roses, filling the house with a beguiling perfume.

In the dining room, tables set with linens and silver and glittering crystal waited to tempt Maria's guests with a cold midnight supper of Low Country delicacies and fine wines.

The house and its decorations were Eden Cade's unique artistry. The tables and their repasts were Cullen's Christmas masterpieces, his gift to Maria.

"It's beautiful." As an enchanted child might, Maria had

explored every inch of the house, touched and admired every decoration. "I didn't realize exactly how beautiful, until now."

"A beautiful setting, a beautiful season." Catching her hands in his, Jericho lifted them to his lips. "A beautiful and generous woman all of Belle Terre will miss."

"Don't." Clasping his hand, she shook her head, setting more fallen tendrils adrift about her shoulders. "Let's not think beyond tonight."

"If that's what you want." Jericho smiled, but with a shadow of sadness in the tilt of his lips. "We'll pretend we're in a time warp, with no tomorrow."

But there would be a tomorrow, and another. The holiday season would end, and Maria would leave. It would be different this time. Nothing had been discussed, her decision was too new, too painful for discussion. Yet Jericho knew their separate lives must touch again. Then, as now, they would pretend there was no tomorrow.

Once he would have gone with her to the ends of the earth. But now he couldn't.

His look strayed to Letitia Rivers. Proud, brave, outspoken, outrageous, failing with age. And Leah, living each day in pain she denied and tried to hide. Pain that would only get worse. Neither would keep him, if given that choice. But neither was as independent as he let her believe.

"No tomorrows," he murmured as the doorbell chimed. Ignoring the ache that banded his heart, standing tall and ruggedly handsome in magnificent black tie, he went with Maria to greet the first of the concert patrons and an added, pleasing mix of guests.

The first to arrive was Daniel Corbett, conductor of the Belle Terre symphony. A man with a soft yet authoritative voice, and laughing eyes. A charismatic and striking man who made the proper remarks and comments, then went immediately to Letitia.

"Oh, dear," Maria murmured. "I hope this doesn't mean

he's going to scold her for her behavior tonight at the concert.''

Rousing from a somber mood, Jericho chuckled faintly. ''Never. Daniel's madly in love with my grandmother.''

''In love!'' Maria looked from Daniel to Jericho. ''Madly?''

''Of course. In fact, he's insanely jealous of me. Because he wishes she were his grandmother.''

''Even though she disrupts his concerts?''

''Especially because she disrupts his concerts. Daniel takes his music seriously, but he's far from a stuffed shirt.''

Wondering if all the people she'd considered the elite of Belle Terre had earthy quirks in their character, Maria greeted the next wave of guests. The newest arrivals were the beginning of a deluge, leaving little time for more than a welcoming exchange.

Adams Cades's brothers were part of the crush. Each as different in looks and personality as any men could be. Lincoln, who was second to Adams, was tall and quiet and pragmatic, as Maria remembered. Next came Jackson, his temperament matching his unruly auburn hair, and still an incorrigible flirt. Last there was Jeffie, with blond hair and dark blue eyes, the softest spoken, the most stunning. The Cades's beloved baby brother.

''No dates?'' Maria questioned as the Cades wandered away.

''There have been ladies in their lives. There will likely be again. But at the moment each is too busy. Lincoln with his veterinary practice, Jackson with his horse farm, and Jefferson with a lot of things. What he does best is paint.''

''Jefferson Cade! Cade, not Cole.'' Maria whispered in dawning recognition. ''Jeffie? Adams's brother painted the marvelous portrait of Eden? I could never make out the painter's name.''

The next wave of guests arrived, and the next, leaving no more time for discussion. Lady's Hall filled, quickly, buzzing with exuberant conversations, punctuated by frequent laughter.

When the last expected guest arrived, Maria and Jericho moved among the shifting, changing throng. Letitia, they discovered, was holding court in the drawing room. Leah had joined a group of couples. Some of whom Maria remembered from the past, some from Jericho's introductions in the foyer.

Eden and Adams had found a quiet alcove, with Eden looking tired, triumphant and content. The party was in Cullen's hands now.

Tom Sims, dressed in the formal wear of a waiter, moved through the house with a tray of wines and champagne.

"Tom," Maria exclaimed. "What are you doing here?"

"Double shifts at the park and serving as the Rivers's chauffeur doesn't keep you busy enough?" Jericho asked. "Or did you get pressed into service?"

"I volunteered, Sheriff. Mrs. Cade and Miss Delacroix have been so good to Joey, I wanted to help out."

"Where is Joey tonight?"

"He's staying at the inn with Merrie, the young maid from Argentina, Miss Delacroix. He likes her stories about gauchos."

"Tell him I'll come by the park before I leave." Maria raised her voice to be heard over the clamor of nearby conversations. "I have a coloring book of marsh and shore birds for him."

A woman squeezed by, jostling Tom's arm. Quick reflexes saved the glasses, but wine splashed over his sleeve. He didn't care. "Then the rumors are true? You're really leaving?"

"My job's finished here." Maria gestured to the room and the house. "So is this project. It's time to move on."

"But I thought..." Tom's look flickered to Jericho's arm circling Maria's waist, making it plain what he thought.

"Why?" the younger man demanded. "I thought you were happy. That you finally felt safe here. What will happen to this house?"

Jericho grasped Tom's arm in a hard grip. "You're overstepping. Maria Elena's plans are none of your business."

At Tom's stricken look, Maria interceded. "I don't mind explaining why I'm leaving, or about the future of the house."

"You're sure?" Jericho asked, his grip never easing.

"I'm sure." Jericho took his hand away, and though she didn't understand Tom's concern, Maria gave the excuse she and Jericho had agreed on days before. "I've enjoyed my extended stay in Belle Terre, but I've made a life and a career on the West Coast, Tom. It's time I got back to both.

"Lady's Hall was a project, a magnificent old house to save. I never intended to live here. The reason for this gathering is to make an official presentation to the hospital. Lady's Hall will serve as lodgings for out-of-town families with critically ill children admitted to the pediatric wing.

"As for feeling safe—" Her voice broke, destroying the blasé spirit she'd striven to create. "Does anyone? Anywhere?"

Tom stared at the floor. The tray forgotten, he spoke in a strained voice. "Safe, Miss Delacroix? I guess not." Glasses rang like wind chimes as his hand shook. "Joey will miss you," he muttered. "So will I." Abruptly, with no apology, he hurried away.

"What do you make of that?" Jericho watched, curiosity stirring, as Tom Sims blended into the crowd.

"It was strange, to say the least." Maria set her glass aside. Suddenly she felt queasy and had no taste for wine.

"Damned strange," Jericho mused, his mind racing. "Another thing that's curious—despite a substantial raise, he's working more jobs, and longer hours. When does he sleep?"

"Maybe there's something Joey wants for Christmas." With a hand she tried to steady, to keep Jericho from noticing her distress, she brushed a sheen of moisture from her throat. "Even if it's something too expensive, Tom would try to manage it."

Jericho pondered her idea. "Makes sense. Joey's sharp, though. He's bound to be aware of their strained finances."

"He's five, Jericho. Five-year-olds still believe in Santa Claus. In that case, he *wouldn't* understand."

"I guess not." Maria had created a logical reason for Tom Sims's attitude, but something about it rankled. An experienced lawman's intuition clawed at Jericho's unsettled mind, an improbable thought clicked into place. And didn't seem so improbable, after all.

Checking to be sure Simon's men and his own were still milling among the crowds, still watching over Maria, he touched her arm, bringing her wandering attention back to him. "Growing bored with me already?"

When she gasped, he frowned. "Something wrong, love?"

Smiling almost feverishly, she struggled to lend a hint of truth to a lie. "Just watching the party."

"Then, if you don't mind, I'd like to check on Mother and *Grandmère*. Make sure Daniel hasn't spirited one or both of them away from me." Along the way, he would find a secluded corner to make a call, checking an idea that increasingly made sense.

"Go." Maria covered his hand with hers. "Eden just joined Yancey by the punch bowl. I'd like to speak to them."

Following her gaze, Jericho discovered his old friend, resplendent in exquisite formal wear, motorcycle boots, a fire-engine-red vest, with a matching band holding his hair at his nape. Forcing a laugh, he muttered, "Yancey Hamilton, rebel to the bone. He must have been a pretty sight dressed like that on his Harley."

But it was this rebel he was most grateful to have watching over Maria. Catching Yancey's eyes, with a barely perceptible nod he consigned her to the rebel's unparalleled care. That accomplished, he kissed her cheek. "I'll be back."

Unaware of the exchange, Maria waited until Jericho was out of sight before she moved toward the back door, not the punch bowl. Intent on staying afoot, she made it to the kitchen, never hearing the crash of breaking glass or Yancey's cry for Adams.

The kitchen staff was busy, no one noticed as she stepped onto the veranda. The breeze blowing from the river was a godsend. Leaning on the balustrade, she let it sweep the worst of the sickness away. In the night air, the sweating stopped, her churning stomach eased. Only a trembling weakness remained.

Her legs were so weak she wondered if she could reach a chair, or the steps lying at her feet. Clinging to her support, she listened to indistinguishable sounds of the party filtering to the veranda. Sounds of the people in Belle Terre who had come to Lady's Hall, treating her as if she were one of them.

"Too late," she murmured. "I learned too late."

"Are you all right, Miss Delacroix?"

The voice came from the darkened end of the veranda. A familiar voice she couldn't quite place. Turning to discover who spoke brought with it an intense wave of vertigo. "Who…?"

"It's Tom Sims, Miss Delacroix." Stepping into the light, he moved to her side.

"What are you doing out here, Tom?"

"Mustering up the nerve to talk to you." When she swayed in an effort to look at him, he caught her shoulders. "I think you need to sit down. The steps, or a chair?"

"The closest."

Once she was seated on the top step, he brought her a cup of water from a pitcher on a table near the door. Eden's thoughtful gesture for any who overindulged in food or drink.

"Should I find a doctor?" Tom asked when she set the cup aside. He stood on the walk, three steps below, his concern visible in the light from a kitchen window.

"I'm better, thank you, Tom. I just needed fresh air." She did feel better sitting in the crisp air, away from the crush of excitement. But this was ridiculous. Considering her work with The Watch, a social gathering in her hometown should be a snap. Sure, she'd driven herself for several weeks. But, again, it was nothing when compared to the rigors of Simon's assignment.

After successfully staving off an aguelike shiver, she forced her own quandary aside. "You wanted to talk to me? Is something wrong with Joey?" Compassion swept the malaise from her voice. "How can I help?"

In the shaft of light that fell over him, she saw his face contort in despair. Alarmed, she cried, "What is it?"

"You." Tom stared at her, seeing only her profile and the drift of her hair as the light at her back turned her into a living shadow. "Since you've been here, your first concern has been how you could help, or what you could for any of us. When there are those of us you should hate."

"That isn't true, Tom. When I came, I was only passing through. When I stayed, it was to find someone who hurt me. For vengeance." *Then I changed,* Maria thought, *because of Jericho.*

She'd known for years that she'd grown hard and unfeeling. On assignments she'd recorded pain with her camera, but never truly felt the hurt. Yet, her time with Josef moved her, as little had in a long time. She realized now that it was because Jericho had touched her and loved her, waking a sleeping heart.

"Why are you leaving?"

Why? Jericho was right, it was no concern of Tom's, but she was too tired to evade. "Because it's best for everyone. I don't want to be the cause of harm to anyone else."

"You won't."

"You don't know that, Tom."

He took a step toward her, his face contorted. "I do know. That's what I've come to tell you."

Maria had leaned her head in her hands, now she straightened. The premonition that she wouldn't like what she was going to hear was as sickening as the vertigo.

"You don't have to be afraid, Miss Delacroix. You never truly needed to be afraid of me."

"Of you?" A chill skittered down her spine, her throat tightened. "What are you saying?"

"Exactly what you think I'm saying."

"You bombed my car?" This was a dream. Tom, the caring, gentle father, couldn't be guilty of such violence. "No. It isn't possible. You aren't capable. Joey needs you too much. Joey…"

Maria stopped short, realizing the full scope of what he'd said. The implications. "You were one of the boys," she whispered. "One of the boys who beat me. But you were new in town and barely knew me. Why? Good lord! We were from the same part of town. What did I do to deserve what you did?"

Her questions tumbled out in a barrage. Oddly, she wasn't frightened, or angry. Only confused, and hurt all over again. "I don't understand. You would have been so young."

"I was twelve, and big for my age."

Only twelve. Not one of the academy boys. It didn't seem possible. But now that she looked at him, seeing more than the harried father, she realized Tom Sims towered over everyone, except Jericho and Cullen. "It was your mask I tore off."

"Yes."

"I didn't recognize you, because I didn't know you."

"We'd passed in the street. No more."

Maria's voice grew calmer, stronger. "But you thought I might recognize you eighteen years later."

"Ridiculous," Tom agreed. "But I couldn't take the chance."

"Because of Joey." He nodded, and Maria saw he was trembling. "What about the others?"

"I'm all that's left. One was killed in an auto accident. One in a knife fight. My brother, Tony, died in Desert Storm. You fell victim to a random gang initiation, Miss Delacroix. But, for that deed, we all got our just deserts. One way or another."

"You think what happened to Joey is your punishment?"

"Maybe. Maybe not." He stood like a statue, but with the trembling more pronounced. "Sins of the father."

"Why are you telling me this now?"

"Because any fool could see how it was between you and Sheriff Rivers then. Even a twelve-year-old fool. Old fools and young fools alike can see now. I've taken enough from you with a violent act. I won't take any more. For the record, Miss Delacroix, when I got home that night, I swore I'd never hurt anyone again.

"And I didn't. Until the car, and the bomb. For that, I'll be eternally sorry."

Too much had happened, too fast. With the dizziness, Maria couldn't take it all in. "What do you want from me now?"

"Nothing. If you'll trust me until tomorrow, I'll go down to the station and tell the sheriff everything I've told you."

"Why tomorrow?"

"I'd like to spend a little time with Joey. Explain some things to him. Make some arrangements."

"What will become of Joey now?"

"The folks who come to the park love Joey. I'm hoping one will take him. Maybe teach him to be a better man than his dad."

Tom Sims took a step toward her, his hand outstretched, when a low and deadly voice cleaved the night. "That's far enough, Sims. One more step and you're dead."

"Jericho!" Maria was on her feet, lurching toward the menacing apparition that moved across the lawn. "He won't hurt me."

"No. He won't hurt you." Jericho stepped into a pool of light, his gray eyes glinting. Only a fool would doubt he was death waiting to strike. "Not a second time."

"You heard?" Maria stood as she was. Too fearful for Jericho, and for Tom, to move.

"I heard." From the quiet place he'd made his call, Jericho had overheard the confession, and come, covertly, to Maria's aid. Now his cold stare never left Tom. "Every damned word."

"Then you know Tom won't hurt me, and he won't renege on his promise to come in tomorrow."

"You're asking me to trust him?" Jericho was incredulous. "You of all people, Maria Elena?"

Maria couldn't explain. But she hadn't a doubt Tom Sims would do as he promised. "Yes, I'm asking you to trust Tom."

A muscle rippled in Jericho's cheek, shadow painted a grim mask of anger, disbelief, and disappointment on his face. He started to speak, then hesitated, for once irresolute.

"Miss Maria." Cullen burst through the door, taking the decision from both of them. "Miss Eden has been taken to the hospital. She's asking for you."

Maria took a hurried step and almost lost her balance. Only Jericho's hand steadied her as she asked, "Is she in labor?"

"No." Cullen's voice broke. "She slipped on spilled food. Her head hit the hearth."

The first scream of a siren drowned out anything more Cullen might say. But Maria had heard all she needed to hear. "Let me go, Jericho. Eden needs me."

"Cullen, tell Adams and Eden we'll follow them to the hospital." Jericho had heard the chaos in the dining room, but his need to reach Maria, then the scene in the yard, had driven it from his mind. Now he held her fast, turning to Tom Sims. "I'm going with Maria Elena to the hospital, Sims. Because it's what she wants, I'm trusting you. Until tomorrow. Be at the station, seven sharp. Or I'll come after you. If I do, you'll regret it."

Jericho didn't waste words with another threat. Sensing a puzzling frailty in Maria, with his arm about her, he led her up the steps, then through the eerily quiet house. The lights of the ambulance winked from sight as he put her in his car and followed.

* * *

"How is she?" Returning to the hospital waiting room, Jericho draped his jacket around Maria's shoulders. His duties dispatched by telephone, he sat by her, taking her cold hand in his.

"The doctor thinks it's only a concussion. As a precaution, he ordered tests and X rays."

"Adams is with her?"

"He wouldn't leave her. His brothers and Yancey tried to persuade him to go with them to the cafeteria for breakfast, but he won't budge. The Cades are going to check on their father and the horses. But Yancey's as stubborn as Adams about leaving. When Eden slipped, he broke her fall. Maybe he even saved her life. But in his mind, he didn't do enough, and Eden shouldn't be hurt."

Jericho understood Adams and Yancey completely. Through the long hours of waiting, the scene with Tom Sims played over and over in his mind, a horror movie without an end. If Tom had been a different sort, Maria could have been lost to him.

"Maria Elena." When she turned, her gaze questioning, he smiled. "It was nothing. I'm just glad you're here."

"Tom never intended to harm me, Jericho."

"I know." But, what if he had intended it? Given the opportunity Sims had, what could anyone have done to stop him?

"Where were you just now?" Maria asked.

"I made some calls. Checked on Mother and *Grandmère*. Joey's with them. Tom turned himself in just after dawn. It's a helluva way for a kid to spend Christmas Eve. Away from home, his dad in jail."

"Will he stay there?" Yancey stood in the door, his face as grim and haggard as Adams's had been.

"I doubt he could make bail," Jericho said. "But there are extenuating circumstances."

"Such as?" Yancey's tone held none of his trademark drawl.

"Such as he was paying Toby Parker's medical bills and

any other expenses the kid accumulated due to the injuries he suffered in the bombing. Anonymously, he thought. At first, all I had to go on was Tom's attitude and the fact that his raise hadn't changed his life. In fact, he worked harder and stayed poor.

"After speaking with the parents, I was convinced. Then, this morning, Tom admitted as much to Court."

Yancey's level gaze narrowed. "Might help when he goes to trial. That, and proof he's been a straight arrow for eighteen years. Too bad he went a little crazy when Maria came home.

"Probably would have taken his chances even then, if it hadn't been for his own kid. Didn't count on the punk."

"Are the parents angry?" Maria asked.

"No. Yancey was right when he called him a punk. He's been in one predicament after another for the past two years." Jericho frowned, remembering. "His folks are good people, but they're older, and couldn't control him. The way they see it, this might be a blessing in disguise. A lesson diverting disaster."

"They won't be pressing charges," Yancey surmised.

"Not unless they have a change of heart." Jericho stood, then prowled restlessly, something plainly on his mind.

"Complicated case," Yancey suggested.

"Yeah," Jericho muttered. "From a twelve-year-old batterer to a fourteen-year-old car thief. With years of pain between."

"And Joey," Maria added into the mix.

Jericho sighed. "And Joey, who may lose his only parent."

"Sims could get probation," Yancey suggested. "If nothing else comes up to complicate it."

A swinging door opened, and Adams came striding through. His jacket was gone, his black tie hung limply from the open collar of his shirt. He was disheveled and exhausted, and exuberant. "She's okay. The headache's subsided, her vision's clearing."

His smiled turned to a grin. "Now she's in labor. Healthy

labor, and right on time. It's Christmas Eve morning. Looks like we'll have our Christmas girl, after all.

"She wants to see you, Maria. She knows about Tom and she wants to make sure you're okay."

Adams paused again, staring blankly as if there was more he should do. Then he snapped his fingers. "Cullen! I've gotta call Cullen. He'll be tossing out the holiday guests to get over here, if I don't. He's already decided he's going to give Caesar Augustus Cade a run for his money in the grandpa department."

Adams had picked up the waiting room telephone and dialed, before Yancey drawled, "Gus Cade, meanest bastard and toughest father this side of the Atlantic, dandling a baby girl on his knee?"

Hunkering down for the rest of the long wait friends would spend with a friend, with brows arched over green eyes brilliant with laughter for the first time in six hours, the handsome rebel of Belle Terre muttered, "This I gotta see."

Epilogue

The little knoll was cloistered in darkness—only moonlight showed the way as Maria and Jericho strolled hand-in-hand across the grass. At a small grave known only in their hearts, they stopped.

"Did you think we would stand here like this again?" Maria asked, her voice filled with the wonder of recent days.

"Never." Jericho admitted. "But would we be here if so many things hadn't fallen into place as if this were meant to be? Some of them mistakes." He remembered. "Some, good fortune. Even Eden's accident provided the rare distraction of Simon's men and my own. The momentary lapse that could have been tragic allowed a man we would never have suspected the chance to steal time alone with you to confess."

"What will happen to him, Jericho? Will the judge take a good life into account, as Yancey thought might be done?"

"Maybe. So long as nothing else comes up."

"So long as nothing else comes up," Maria mused, then fell silent for a time. Finally, quietly, she spoke again. "He isn't really a bad man. In fact, the foolish boy I thought I would hate is a good man and a good father. Joey would be devastated without him.''

Jericho waited, hearing her out.

Maria's hand gripped his harder, tighter. ''We don't really know for sure why we lost our baby, do we?''

Jericho understood where she was going with this. He knew it was for Joey, not Tom. ''No, sweetheart, we don't.''

''Then she needn't become an instrument of vengeance?''

His law degree had gathered dust for years. Even if it hadn't, with time and minors complicating the issues, the situation would need study. But in Jericho's mind, none of that mattered. This was their decision to make, not the court's. Only theirs, and Maria's more than his. ''We don't have to do anything you don't want to do. Or say anything you don't want to say.''

Maria smiled. A brilliant, breathtaking smile with no hint of the anguish of their past. For Jericho it marked the beginning of a new life without bitterness, or vengeance. A new life to share.

Moving a little apart, Maria looked beyond the knoll. Belle Terre lay there, the houses dark as the city slept. ''I misjudged most of them. I realize now I was as guilty of prejudging as anyone.''

In the quiet, a distant clock struck twice. Reminding them of the time, and the day. Trailing her fingers over the stone that read simply Baby Girl, Maria looked up at him. Her smile trembled. ''Listen, Jericho, it's Christmas morning. Adams and Eden have their little girl. And we have each other. This time, forever.''

Jericho opened his arms. Moonlight shone on the gold band on his right hand where he would keep it, honoring a love grown stronger with time. When she came to him, her own band tinkling at her wrist, he murmured, ''Then shall we go home, Mrs. Rivers?''

''Yes.'' There was much left to resolve—like the official

announcement of their marriage. Which Maria was certain Letitia and Leah would delight in handling. After all, she was just as certain, they had been her allies before. First, with tuition to the academy, as Lady Mary's anonymously benevolent friends. Then with the invitation to the holiday concert, and a dress of silver lace.

Perhaps they would help make Maxie's quiet benevolence a constant reality. Maria couldn't think of anyone who would do as well in continuing his kindnesses.

But that would come later. First, before anything, she must tell Jericho she was sure Eden's little girl would soon have a playmate. There could never be another summer girl. But her sister, or her brother, wouldn't be any less wanted, any less loved.

Touching the turquoise heart, Jericho's gift to her, Maria laughed softly. He'd given her a talisman for wishes. Wishes that came true. Now she knew what gifts she would give him. First her own heart, a heart filled with love. A heart without anger.

And then…the best of all gifts.

"Let's go home, Jericho. Our baby girl can sleep in peace now, and we have much to be thankful for. So much to celebrate." Rising on tiptoe, she drew him down to her, brushing his lips with hers, making promises to keep. For now, for tomorrow. Forever.

"This is our first Christmas," she whispered at last. "And I have something wonderful to tell you."

* * * * *

Look for more
MEN OF BELLE TERRE
from Silhouette Desire in 2001.

January 2001
TALL, DARK & WESTERN
#1339 by Anne Marie Winston

February 2001
THE WAY TO A RANCHER'S HEART
#1345 by Peggy Moreland

March 2001
MILLIONAIRE HUSBAND
#1352 by Leanne Banks
Million-Dollar Men

April 2001
GABRIEL'S GIFT
#1357 by Cait London
Freedom Valley

May 2001
THE TEMPTATION OF
RORY MONAHAN
#1363 by Elizabeth Bevarly

June 2001
A LADY FOR LINCOLN CADE
#1369 by BJ James
Men of Belle Terre

MAN OF THE MONTH

For twenty years Silhouette has been giving
you the ultimate in romantic reads. Come join
the celebration as some of your favorite authors
help celebrate our anniversary with the most
sensual, emotional love stories ever!

Available at your favorite retail outlet.

Where love comes alive™

#1 *New York Times* bestselling author

NORA ROBERTS

brings you more of the loyal and loving, tempestuous and tantalizing Stanislaski family.

Coming in February 2001

The Stanislaski Sisters

Natasha and Rachel

Though raised in the Old World traditions of their family, fiery Natasha Stanislaski and cool, classy Rachel Stanislaski are ready for a *new* world of love....

And also available in February 2001 from Silhouette Special Edition, the newest book in the heartwarming Stanislaski saga

CONSIDERING KATE

Natasha and Spencer Kimball's daughter Kate turns her back on old dreams and returns to her hometown, where she finds the *man* of her dreams.

Available at your favorite retail outlet.

Silhouette®

where love comes alive—online...

eHARLEQUIN.com

your romantic escapes

Indulgences

♥ Monthly guides to indulging yourself, such as:
  - ★ Tub Time: A guide for bathing beauties
  - ★ Magic Massages: A treat for tired feet

Horoscopes

♥ Find your daily Passionscope, weekly Lovescopes and Erotiscopes

♥ Try our compatibility game

Reel Love

♥ Read all the latest romantic movie reviews

Royal Romance

♥ Get the latest scoop on your favorite royal romances

Romantic Travel

♥ For the most romantic destinations, hotels and travel activities

If you enjoyed what you just read,
then we've got an offer you can't resist!

Take 2 bestselling love stories FREE!

Plus get a FREE surprise gift!

COMING NEXT MONTH

#1339 TALL, DARK & WESTERN—Anne Marie Winston
Man of the Month
Widowed rancher Marty Stryker needed a wife for his young daughter, so he placed an ad in the paper. When attractive young widow Juliette Duchenay answered his ad, the chemistry between them was undeniable. Marty knew he was falling for Juliette, but could he risk his heart for a second chance at love and family?

#1340 MILLIONAIRE M.D.—Jennifer Greene
Texas Cattleman's Club: Lone Star Jewels
When Winona Raye discovered a baby girl on her doorstep, wealthy surgeon Justin Webb proposed a marriage of convenience to give the child a family. But for Winona, living under the same roof with the sexy doctor proved to be a challenge. Because now that Justin had the opportunity to get close to Winona, he was determined to win her heart.

#1341 SHEIKH'S WOMAN—Alexandra Sellers
Sons of the Desert
Anna Lamb woke with no memory of her newborn baby, or of the tall, dark and handsome sheikh who claimed to be her husband. Although she was irresistibly drawn to Ishaq Ahmadi, Anna couldn't understand his anger and suspicion until the sheikh revealed his identity...and his shocking reasons for claiming *her* as his woman....

#1342 THE BARONS OF TEXAS: KIT—Fayrene Preston
The Barons of Texas
Kit Baron was in serious trouble. One of her ranch hands was dead, and she was the only suspect. Then criminal lawyer Des Baron—the stepcousin Kit had always secretly loved— came to her rescue. Now he was determined to prove her innocence, but could Kit prove her love for Des?

#1343 THE EARL'S SECRET—Kathryn Jensen
When American tour guide Jennifer Murphy met the dashing young Earl Christopher Smythe in Scotland, sparks flew. Before long their relationship became a passionate affair and Jennifer fell in love with Christopher. But the sexy earl had a secret, and in order to win the man of her dreams, Jennifer would have to uncover the truth....

#1344 A COWBOY, A BRIDE & A WEDDING VOW—Shirley Rogers
Cowboy Jake McCall never knew he was a father until Catherine St. John's son knocked on his door. In order to get to know his son, Jake convinced Catherine to stay on his ranch for the summer. Could the determined cowboy rekindle the passion between them and persuade Catherine to stay a lifetime?

CMN1200